Dreaming
by
Starlight

SIOBHAN CURHAM

WALKER
BOOKS

First published 2022 by Walker Books Ltd
87 Vauxhall Walk, London SE11 5HJ

2 4 6 8 10 9 7 5 3 1

© 2022 Siobhan Curham

Cover illustration © 2022 Kate Forrester

This book has been typeset in Berolina, Arial, AT Arta and Clarendon

Printed and bound by CPI Group (UK) Ltd, Croydon, CR0 4YY

British Library Cataloguing in Publication Data: a catalogue record for this book is available from the British Library

ISBN 978-1-5295-0401-9

www.walker.co.uk

*This book is dedicated to all of the loyal
readers of the first Moonlight Dreamers books.
Your passion for the series has meant the world to me.*

"We are all in the gutter, but some of us are looking at the stars." – Oscar Wilde

Chapter One

Jazz knew that it was wrong to sulk. She knew – thanks to Grace Love, her favourite Instagram influencer – that being resentful towards someone was like drinking poison and hoping the other person would die, but she was pretty sure that strangling your parents was illegal in the UK, just as it was in Australia, so what else could she do?

"Are you sure you don't want any, Jazz?" her mum, Cheryl, asked, picking up the silver platter of pilau rice. It looked delicious, the plump grains glowing yellow and gold in the light of the flickering candle at the centre of the table. But Jazz shook her head. Normally she loved Indian food, and the warm aroma of spices filling the restaurant was making her mouth water, but she mustn't give in. If she ate anything, it would look as if she was admitting defeat in the battle of wills against her parents.

"How about a piece of naan?" Her uncle Gerald gestured at the basket of equally delicious-looking bread. "They make the best here, it's as light as a cloud!"

Trying to ignore her rumbling stomach, Jazz shook her head once more. Gerald was her dad's older brother. There were fifteen years between them and in many ways they were complete opposites. Gerald had cropped white hair, whereas Mikey's fell in dark waves to his shoulders – although if she looked closely she could see the beginnings of a sprinkling of grey at his temples. Gerald spoke like a Shakespearean actor, enunciating every word as if he were delivering a soliloquy, but Mikey's British accent had been softened by an Australian twang after years living on the Gold Coast. The only thing they did have in common were their jobs in the arts: Gerald was an artist and Mikey was a music producer.

This was only the second time Jazz had met Gerald. The first had been eight years ago, when she was six, and he and Daniel, his husband, had come to visit them in Sydney with their daughter, Amber.

Amber had changed so much, Jazz thought as she looked across the table at her cousin. Jazz's abiding memory from their visit had been one of huge disappointment. She'd been so looking forward to meeting her big cousin from London, imagining them playing on the beach and in the ocean together. But Amber had spent most of her time with her nose in a book, and when her dads had made her come to the beach, she'd complained endlessly about not wanting to get sunburnt. Now, at eighteen, Amber's pale, wiry frame formed part of a really cool look, complete with damson-coloured hair, cut in a short, sharp bob, and a men's pin-striped suit.

Amber caught Jazz's gaze and raised her thin dark eyebrows, as if asking whether she was all right. Even as Jazz nodded, she felt floored by a sudden, overwhelming sense of loss as the distance between her and her friends back home hit her. When her parents had broken the news that they were moving to the UK, Jazz had gone into a state of shock. Their decision had been final, with no consideration for Jazz's feelings, Cheryl telling her that they needed to move for her dad's career. Jazz couldn't understand why her mum had been such a willing accomplice in such a terrible plan. Like Jazz, she'd lived all her life in Australia; surely she had just as much to lose? But her mum had kept repeating the same old mantra: *We need to do it for your dad, for our family.*

At the table, Cheryl laughed loudly at something Daniel had said. In normal circumstances, if Jazz hadn't been so full of rage at everyone and everything, she would have liked Amber's other dad. His tanned skin and athletic build reminded her of the surfers back home and he had a really positive energy about him.

"More wine, guys?" Jazz's dad asked, as he gestured at one of the waiters to come over.

"Absolutely!" Gerald agreed. "Although I think we should try a French Chardonnay this time. Can't beat a French vino."

The bitter seed of resentment in the pit of Jazz's empty stomach began growing tendrils, filling her until she was barely able to swallow. She picked up her fork and prodded at a piece of chicken. This was so unfair. It was easy for adults to move around the world, especially if they were doing it for work, like her dad, but Jazz was fourteen. She was still stuck in school. Her mouth went dry at the thought of starting a brand-new school in a brand-new country *next week*. They'd been in their new home in Brighton for only a fortnight and hadn't had the chance to meet anyone yet.

Much to her horror her eyes filled with tears and, before she could do anything to stop it, one rolled down her cheek. She quickly wiped it away. Thankfully none of the adults noticed; they were far too busy having a jokey argument about which was best, French or Australian Chardonnay. She felt something tap her foot beneath the table and looked up to see Amber staring at her.

Are you OK? she mouthed.

Jazz gulped. More tears were threatening. This was so embarrassing.

"I – I just need to go to the bathroom," she stammered, getting to her feet.

Somehow Jazz managed to weave her way through the crowded restaurant to the door at the back marked toilets. It opened on to a steep, narrow staircase and she hurried down the steps and into the ladies', where she locked herself inside one of the two cubicles. The air was cooler down there and smelled of floral air freshener.

Jazz leaned against the wall and took a deep breath. But it was no good, the grief welling inside her was too huge to suppress. She put her face in her hands and began to sob. She couldn't even message any of her friends because the time difference meant that it was 5 a.m. in Sydney. London may as well be on a different planet. The toilet door opened and someone came in. Jazz quickly grabbed some tissues and dabbed at her eyes.

"Are you all right?" a girl's voice — Amber's — asked from the other side of the cubicle door.

"Oh — yes — I'm — I'm fine," Jazz stammered. *Crap!* She wiped away her tears.

"I was just wondering if you'd like to come for a walk?" Amber said. "I don't know about you, but there's only so long I can listen to the oldies drone on about wine before I want to curl up and die from boredom."

Jazz couldn't help laughing.

"Plus there's something I'd like to share with you," Amber added.

The sorrow engulfing Jazz began to fade a little. She pressed the flush to make it look as if she'd been going to the toilet rather than having a meltdown, then opened the cubicle door.

"Sounds good," she muttered, without making eye contact. Hopefully Amber wouldn't notice she'd been crying.

"Excellent!"

Jazz followed Amber up into the restaurant. She could hear her parents' laughter as soon as they got back upstairs. It seemed so unfair that they could be so happy when she felt so low.

"We're just going to go for a walk," Amber said when they reached the table. She must have said something to them beforehand as the adults all looked up and nodded and smiled, and Cheryl didn't even mention the fact that Jazz had barely touched her dinner.

Jazz grabbed her jacket from the back of her chair. "See you later," she mumbled, before following Amber out of the door.

Chapter Two

The September air was crisp and cool and the narrow pavement buzzed with all kinds of people, from sharply dressed businessmen and women to quirkily dressed students and photo-hungry tourists. According to Mikey, when he'd been trying to sell Jazz on the idea of coming to visit Amber and her parents, Brick Lane was one of the hippest streets in London. Apparently it was *the* place to go for a curry, due to the plethora of Indian restaurants owned by the local Bangladeshi community. And, according to her dad, it had an "awesome creative vibe" thanks to the hipsters who'd taken over the nearby neighbourhood of Shoreditch.

Jazz didn't want to be impressed. Her eyes sought out more reasons to feel deflated, like the tide of litter gathering by the kerb, the homeless man sitting and staring blankly in the doorway of an abandoned shop, the waiters standing on the pavement in their crisp white shirts and black trousers, trying to persuade passers-by to dine at their restaurants.

"So, how are you doing – really?" Amber asked, coming to a stop outside a store.

Before Jazz could reply, a man walking by jostled into her. Normally this would have prompted her to deliver a witty retort like, *Did you leave your manners at home, mate?* But it was as if a different person had boarded the plane to the UK, leaving the fun-loving, feisty person she used to be back in Sydney. There was no point lying to Amber but she didn't want to seem like a whiny baby either.

"I just — I miss my friends."

Amber smiled sympathetically. "I'm not surprised you're feeling mumpish."

"Feeling what?"

"Sorry, that was my word of the day from eighteenth-century-dictionary-dot-com. It means gloomy."

"Oh, I see." Jazz laughed. "Yep, I'm definitely feeling a bit mumpish."

"Well, don't worry." Amber said. "I might be able to help."

"Really?" Jazz felt a glimmer of hope. Did Amber want to be friends with her? But then she remembered something her mum had said on the way up to London, something about Amber going to work in a bookshop in Paris. Jazz's head had been buzzing with so many angry thoughts at the time that she couldn't remember the exact details.

"First I'm going to buy you something to eat before you wilt away. You hardly touched your dinner. And I know how annoying it can be when you refuse to eat to teach your parents a lesson but then they have the last laugh because you end up starving."

"That's not what I was doing."

Amber looked her in the eye. "Really?"

Jazz laughed. "OK, maybe a little."

"I knew it!" Amber grinned. "And of all the places to do it. Gerald wasn't exaggerating about that naan bread, you really missed a treat. But don't worry, I know the next best thing."

She turned and headed into a store. The sign above the doorway read BLUEBIRD BURFI. Jazz gazed at the counter in front of her. It was full of trays of what looked like some kind of sweets, in the most beautiful shades of pink, yellow, orange and green. The shop smelled delicious too, a sugary, creamy aroma, with a hint of cinnamon.

"Amber!" a girl cried from behind the counter. Her skin was pale brown and her long black hair shone beneath the twinkling lights on the ceiling. She was wearing a traditional Indian dress in bright pistachio green.

"Hey, Maali. This is my cousin, Jazz."

"It's so lovely to meet you." Maali extended her slim arm over the counter. Her wrist was full of delicate gold bangles that jingled as she shook Jazz's hand.

"Thanks. You too," Jazz replied.

"She's the one I was telling you about," Amber continued. "The one who's moved here from Australia."

"Wow," Maali exclaimed. "That's a long way to come."

"Yeah, I've just about got rid of the jetlag, two weeks later," Jazz joked.

As Amber and Maali chatted away about what they'd been doing, Jazz watched the people hurrying by outside and, once again, she was overwhelmed by the feeling of not belonging. It was like being part of a highly choreographed dance routine where everyone knew their steps apart from her. She tuned back in to the other girls' conversation. Amber was asking for something called golden milk and a box of burfi.

"What's golden milk?" Jazz asked.

"It is the elixir of the gods, the nectar of the heavens," Amber replied dreamily. "It's—"

"It's basically warm almond milk with turmeric and other spices," Maali interrupted with a grin.

"It's a hug in a cup," Amber continued.

Maali giggled. "Oh Amber, you're so funny." She took a white cardboard box from a shelf behind her and, using a pair of silver tongs, started filling it with cubes of the sweets on display. Much to Jazz's surprise her mouth began to water and she started to feel light-headed with hunger. She'd been so depressed lately she thought her appetite had gone for good. Maali disappeared into the back of the store, reappearing a couple of minutes later holding two takeaway cups.

"Thanks, Maals." As Amber leaned over the counter to hug her friend Jazz felt another wistful pang. The way they chatted to each other was so easy-going and informal, filled with the kind of conversational shortcuts that only came from years of friendship.

"So, you're going to tell her about *him*," Maali said to Amber with a knowing grin.

"Yep, I think it's time he helped someone else," Amber replied, and they both turned to Jazz and smiled.

Jazz's face began to burn. She wasn't sure she liked the sound of some mystery guy helping her. She wasn't a charity case. All right, maybe she was, but she didn't want half of London knowing she had no mates.

"Right, let's go to mine," Amber said once they'd said goodbye to Maali and were back outside.

"Aren't we going for a walk?"

"I had to say that to throw the parentals off the scent."

"Oh, I see." The plot thickened.

They turned down a side street lined with three-storey townhouses and lit by old-fashioned lamps. It was like walking onto the set of one of the BBC period dramas Jazz's mum liked to watch. Now that Jazz was free from her parents and her need to punish them with silence, she was able to appreciate that this place was, in fact, pretty cool. The inside of Amber's house was even cooler – kind of like the house Sherlock Holmes lived in, crammed full of antique furniture, including a grandfather clock ticking loudly in the hall.

When Jazz and her parents had arrived earlier, they'd only been in the living room and kitchen, but Amber led Jazz past them and up a winding old wooden staircase, taking two steps at a time.

"'Scuse the mess," Amber said, ushering her into a room

at the very top of the house. "I'm having trouble deciding what to pack for Paris."

Like the rest of the house, the room was full of antique furniture but Amber had added her own original touches. Posters from plays papered the walls and a four-poster bed was covered in a colourful patchwork quilt and a family of different-sized Moroccan-style cushions. By the window, an intricately carved wooden desk spilled over with books, notepads and papers, while more books lined the alcoves either side of the fireplace. In one corner of the room an old record player perched on top of a trunk and a mound of vintage clothes lay on the floor. Jazz could just make out the handle of a suitcase protruding from underneath. A teetering pile of yet more books stood beside it.

"It seems pretty stupid to take so many books, given that I'm going to be living in a bookstore for the next year." Amber sighed.

"You're going to be living *in* the store?"

"Yes. It's this magical shop in Paris called Shakespeare and Company and they allow young writers to live and work there. They have little bunks tucked away among the shelves." Amber smiled dreamily. "Just think of it – falling asleep surrounded by all of those stories!"

"Sounds awesome," Jazz replied, although to be truthful it wasn't her idea of bliss. She'd never been much of a bookworm. She found it hard to sit still long enough to get beyond a paragraph.

"Right, we're going to need this." Amber took a small, leather-bound book down from one of the shelves. "And this." She went over to the desk and fetched a velvet bag from one of the drawers. "Let's go up to the roof garden. Hopefully we'll be able to see it."

"See what?"

"The moon."

Jazz stared after her blankly. Nothing that Amber had done so far made any sense. She'd told their parents they were going on a walk, but instead she'd taken Jazz to a shop to get some food – food that they still hadn't eaten – then she and Maali had talked mysteriously about some random guy, and now she was going on about the moon. There'd better not be some beardy old astronomer waiting for them up there! She hurried after her down a narrow passageway to a door, which Amber unlocked with a large iron key.

"Ta-da!" she exclaimed.

In an instant, all of the tension Jazz had been feeling melted away.

"This is ace!" she gasped as she looked around the roof garden crammed with brightly coloured ceramic pots containing plants of all shapes and sizes. Fairy lights lit up the walls surrounding the garden and beyond that the London skyline twinkled in the gathering darkness.

"It's my haven away from annoying parents – or one particularly annoying parent," Amber added with a chuckle.

"Which one?" Jazz asked.

"Gerald." Amber rolled her eyes. "He can be insufferable."

"Must be a sibling thing," Jazz muttered – maybe Gerald and Mikey had more than their jobs in common after all.

"You don't get on with Uncle Mikey?" Amber asked.

"Not any more."

"Since the move?"

Jazz nodded. "He doesn't seem to care how hard it is for me."

"Yep, that sounds familiar." Amber led her over to some garden chairs grouped round a table in the corner. "Don't tell me, his precious job comes before everything?"

"Yes!"

The two girls looked at each other and laughed. This was the most relaxed Jazz had felt since leaving Australia. Why did Amber have to be moving away?

They sat down at the table and Amber cleared her throat. "Have you tried your drink yet?"

Jazz hadn't. She brought the cup to her lips and took a sip. The golden milk tasted delicious. Creamy and sweet without being sickly. "Oh wow."

"I know, right?" Amber grinned. "Wait till you try a piece of burfi." She opened the cardboard box and offered it to her.

Jazz took one of the orange cubes.

"Good choice," Amber said. "That was our friend Rose's creation. Orange and cardamom."

Jazz sat back in her chair as the burfi melted on her tongue, filling her mouth with the most delicious combination of flavours.

"So, I'm sure you've heard of a writer called Oscar Wilde."

Jazz looked at her blankly and Amber's face fell.

"He … uh … sounds familiar," Jazz said quickly.

"So he should. He's one of the finest writers ever to have lived."

So the mystery guy Amber and Maali had been talking about was a writer. Jazz silently groaned. Was Amber about to invite her to join some kind of book club? She didn't want to disappoint Amber, though. She needed to look enthusiastic.

"Is he on Instagram?" she asked, taking her phone out.

"No!" Amber exclaimed, her mouth gaping open in horror. "He died over a hundred years ago."

Jazz's face flushed and she slid her phone back in her pocket. Hopefully it was too dark for Amber to notice.

"You can still find loads of quotes by him all over the internet, though," Amber added with a warm smile. "And in books like this." She gestured to the book she'd got down from the shelf in her room. "Oscar was the inspiration behind something I set up when I was your age and I didn't … well … I didn't really have any friends," Amber continued. "It's how I got to know Maali, and Sky and Rose, and they became the best friends I could have wished for."

"Oh," Jazz replied, although she didn't quite follow. "How did – I mean – what was it that you set up?"

"A secret society," Amber replied in a hushed tone.

Jazz frowned. Was this all part of some elaborate prank?

She glanced over her shoulder to check that Maali wasn't lurking, laughing behind the plants.

"It all started with a game I used to play." Amber picked up the book. "It's called What Would Oscar Say? I still play it to this day." She passed the book to Jazz. "Think of something that's on your mind right now – like a question or a problem you need an answer to."

"OK." Jazz pictured her parents laughing and drinking in the restaurant on Brick Lane and the way they didn't seem to care about her feelings. She wondered if she'd ever feel happy again.

"Have you thought of a question?" Amber asked.

Jazz nodded as a question took shape in her head. *How will I ever feel happy again?*

"Now, flick the book open to a random page."

Jazz did as she was told. The page she turned to contained just a couple of lines of writing.

"What does it say?" Amber was looking at her excitedly, her dark eyes sparkling in the glow of the fairy lights.

Jazz held it up to the light and squinted at the page. "It says, 'We are all in the gutter, but some of us are looking at the stars.'"

What, exactly, did that mean?

But Amber was clapping her hands together. "I love that one! And it's so perfect for you."

"It is?"

"Yes! You're feeling low because you've had to move to the UK, right?"

"Right."

"So you could say that your life is in the gutter right now."

"Yes, I guess."

"But you can still choose to look at the stars."

Jazz wanted to ask how looking at the stars was going to help her but she didn't want Amber to think she was stupid.

"Obviously, he's speaking in metaphor," Amber continued. "Saying that you need to keep your focus on the brighter things to come, not on what is actually happening right now."

Jazz thought of what was to come: starting at a new school where she knew no one hardly seemed like a bright prospect.

"You have to visualize your happiest possible future," Amber said, taking another piece of burfi.

"Hmm, no offence but my happiest possible future is back home in Sydney with my friends but, thanks to my dad, that's never going to happen."

"Here," Amber said, offering her the burfi.

"Thank you." Jazz took a pale green piece. "I just – I can't really see how I'm going to be happy."

"And that's exactly why I need to share the secret with you," Amber replied enigmatically.

"What secret?"

"The secret of the Moonlight Dreamers."

Chapter Three

"So, when I was your age and completely and utterly friendless..." Amber began.

I'm not friendless, Jazz thought, defensively. *I have heaps of friends. They're just seventeen thousand kilometres away!*

"... I reached a breaking point. I was up here in the garden when it happened, actually." She looked out at the London skyline and Jazz followed her gaze, hearing the pounding bassline and chatter and laughter drifting up from a bar, and, in the distance, the wail of a siren.

"I was being picked on by some bloviator girls at my school—"

"Bloviator?" Jazz cut in.

"People who love the sound of their own voices but have nothing of any consequence to say."

Jazz grinned. She assumed this was another of Amber's old-fashioned words of the day.

"Anyway, Gerald – well, he was being Gerald," she laughed. "So I played What Would Oscar Say? and the quote I landed on changed everything."

"What was it?" Jazz asked, hoping it wasn't the stars

and gutter one. All that had done was make her feel more miserable.

Amber leafed through the pages of the book and passed it back to her.

"*Yes: I am a dreamer. For a dreamer is one who can only find his way by moonlight, and his punishment is that he sees the dawn before the rest of the world,*" Jazz read. Geez, what was with the moon and stars obsession? Was this Oscar dude a writer or an astrologer? Jazz glanced up and saw that Amber was looking at her expectantly.

"That's great," Jazz replied flatly. She really didn't get how this was supposed to make her feel better.

"Isn't it? So, what do you think it means?"

She thought Amber was supposed to be helping her, not giving her an English Literature lesson. She looked back at the quote.

"Well, he's saying that he's a dreamer…" she began.

"Yes…"

"And he prefers to dream at night?" This was excruciating.

"Why do you think he says that?"

"I don't know. Does he, like, get his best ideas at night?"

"But he's not just saying at night, is he?" Amber looked up into the sky. Jazz followed her gaze to the thin silvery sliver of a crescent moon. She looked back at the quote.

"He uses the moonlight to find his way to his dreams?" This made no sense at all, but Amber started nodding eagerly. Jazz was so relieved to have got something right that she kept going. "And then, because he's up in the moonlight, he also gets to see the dawn before anyone else. But how is that a punishment?" Jazz loved watching the sunrise when she went surfing first thing.

"Maybe it's not," Amber replied.

Jazz frowned. "What, was he being ironic?"

"Possibly."

Jazz sighed. This was tying her mind in knots. "So how did this help you find your friends?"

"After I read that quote, I stood here." Amber went and stood by the edge of the garden, beckoning at Jazz to join her. "And I realized that it was OK to be different; to have dreams that were different. And then I looked out at London and I thought that surely there had to be other people like me out there, other people who dared to be different."

Jazz stared down at the people hurrying by on the street below. She knew for sure that there were other people out there like her. The trouble was, they were on the other side of the world.

"I decided that I would find those people," Amber finished.

"How?"

"I started looking out for girls who I thought might be kindred spirits and then I gave them one of these." She reached inside the velvet bag and pulled out a dog-eared postcard which she passed to Jazz.

Jazz held it to the light.

ARE YOU A MOONLIGHT DREAMER?

- Are you a girl aged between 14 and 16?

- Are you sick of being told how to look, what to do and where to go?

- Do you feel trapped in a world full of fakes?

- Do you dream of freedom and adventure?

- When you read the quote below, what does it mean to you?

"Yes: I am a dreamer. For a dreamer is one who can only find his way by moonlight, and his punishment is that he sees the dawn before the rest of the world."

Send your answer to wildeatheart@googlepost.com to find out if you are a Moonlight Dreamer.

"What, you gave these to random girls?" Jazz stared at her, shocked.

"Yep." Amber smiled. "I gave one to Maali when I bumped into her on Brick Lane and I slipped one in Sky's bag when she bought something in the vintage store I used to work in."

"And they replied to you?"

"Yes, and Sky brought her stepsister Rose to our first meeting. And so the Moonlight Dreamers were born."

"Wasn't it awkward, that first meeting?"

"Oh yes." Amber laughed. "Especially as Sky and Rose hated each other's guts back then! But thankfully we had one important thing in common."

"What?"

"We all had dreams we needed help in achieving." Amber looked at Jazz. "Do you have a dream?"

Yes, to move back to Australia. Jazz bit on her lip.

"Or something you love doing?"

"Surfing," she replied instantly. She felt a pang of sorrow. Her new home here might be by a beach but the sea was freezing and there were no decent waves. The most active thing people seemed to do there was paddleboarding.

"OK, great. So, imagine if you had a group of friends who supported you in your passion for surfing."

I do, but they all live too far away.

As if sensing Jazz's growing despondency, Amber reached inside the velvet bag and pulled out another piece of card.

"This might make it a little clearer." She handed it over for Jazz to read.

MOONLIGHT DREAMERS – THE RULES

1. *The Moonlight Dreamers is a secret society – members must never speak a word of its existence, or what happens at the meetings, to others.*

2. *Meetings will begin with members reciting the "moonlight" quote from Oscar Wilde.*

3. *This quote is the Moonlight Dreamers' motto and must be memorized by members – and NEVER forgotten.*

4. *All members must vow to support the other Moonlight Dreamers in the pursuit of their dreams – always.*

5. *Moonlight Dreamers are proud of being different. Being the same as everyone else is a crime against originality, the human equivalent of magnolia paint.*

6. *Moonlight Dreamers tell one another everything – even the bad stuff. Especially the bad stuff.*

7. *Moonlight Dreamers never, ever give up.*

"Look, I'm not saying you *have* to set up your own group of Moonlight Dreamers," Amber said. "I'm just saying that if you find it hard to make friends when you start at your new school, then this is an option."

Jazz forced herself to smile. She really appreciated Amber caring enough to share this with her but the thought of approaching random girls and asking them if they wanted to join her secret society hardly seemed like the best way to create a good first impression at her new school. Surely it would only single her out – and not in a good way!

Amber put the book and cards in the bag and handed it to her. "To the next generation of Moonlight Dreamers," she said dramatically.

"Er – yeah – sure," Jazz replied, taking the bag, absolutely certain she would never, under any circumstances, use it.

Chapter Four

As Hope picked up the dirty plates from the table outside the café, her stomach lurched. Was there anything more gross than other people's congealed leftovers? It was a well-known fact that the food served in her parents' café, Donuts and Discs, was some of the most delicious in all of Brighton. People loved their light fluffy doughnuts, with their crisp golden coating and weird and wonderful fillings, and came from miles around to try them. But having to scrape the remains from the plates was a whole other story, especially when someone had stubbed out a cigarette in the middle of a glob of rhubarb and custard cream. Hope held her breath to try and avoid the smell of ash. It had been one of the worst days ever. How could it not have been, when it had begun with a tearful farewell to her beloved sister, who'd left for university miles away in Manchester?

Although there were four years between them, Megan was Hope's closest friend and confidante. Their mum, Petra, jokingly called them Night and Day because they were so different, but somehow their differences only made them more compatible. Megan's forceful, outgoing personality helped draw Hope from her shell, and Hope's easy-going, introverted nature had helped calm her older sister during many fiery outbursts. More than anything, she and Meg *got* each other. Hope never felt she had to prove anything when she was with her sister, never felt she was being judged. She could say the weird things that popped into her head – things she would never dare say to other people – and pretend to be madcap characters to make her sister laugh – and Meg *always* laughed at her jokes. Over the summer they'd spent loads of time together and got even closer and Hope had barely seen her classmates. They were more like acquaintances than friends, and she always got the impression they were putting on some kind of act. She never felt able to be her true self with them and she definitely wouldn't now. Her stomach lurched again, but this time it wasn't from the dirty dishes.

Hope stared out across the lagoon. A bank of grey storm clouds was rolling in from the sea, mirroring her growing dread. High above her a seagull circled and wailed. She hurried inside. Her dad, Pete, was cashing up by the till and "Here Comes the Sun" by The Beatles was playing on the record player behind the counter. It was her dad's go-to tune when he was feeling blue. Clearly Hope wasn't the only one in need of cheering up.

"All right, love?" he asked as Hope slipped behind the counter.

"Yeah, just got another couple of tables to clear and then I'll be done."

"Are you sure you don't want me to get them?" He looked at her, concerned.

"I'm *fine*," she snapped, instantly feeling guilty. But her parents' fussing reminded her of something she longed to forget. She dumped the dishes in the kitchen and went back outside. The lagoon was deserted apart from one of the water sports team locking up the boat shed for the night. Then she saw a girl with short blonde hair making her way down the steps from the seafront past the children's play area towards the café.

"Are you guys still open?" she called to Hope. She sounded like she was Australian and she was wearing tracksuit bottoms and a vest top that showed off how tanned and toned she was. The polar opposite of Hope, who felt thinner and paler than ever.

"'Fraid not," she said, but the girl looked so disappointed she added, "But we have a few doughnuts left. I could get you something to take away, if you like?"

The girl grinned. "Thanks."

Hope gathered up the last of the dishes and the girl followed her inside. As soon as Pete saw her, he called, "Sorry, love, we're closed."

"It's OK, Dad, I said she could get some doughnuts to take away." Hope dumped the dishes on the counter and went over to the display cabinet. "We have a cherry and cinnamon or a salted toffee apple left."

"Would it be really bad if I had both?" she replied with a grin. She was definitely Australian. Hope wondered if she was in Brighton on holiday. If so, she couldn't help feeling sorry for her. The weather had been terrible. It must seem rubbish compared to the sunshine and warmth of Australia.

"Of course not." Hope smiled. "You can never have too many doughnuts, in my humble opinion. As Shakespeare once said, 'To doughnut or not to doughnut; that is *never* the question!'" As soon as the joke left her mouth, she cringed. She was hopeless at making conversation with new people. She longed for the easy shorthand she shared with Megan. But thankfully, the girl was still grinning.

"Too right!" She giggled.

"Four pounds, please." Hope put the doughnuts in a paper bag with a serviette and handed them to her.

The girl took some coins from her pocket and studied them before passing them over, as if she wasn't quite sure what they were worth. She cleared her throat and looked at the window. "I don't suppose you want—"

"Right, love, let's get those dishes done and head home," Pete said, choosing another record from the collection. Hope knew without looking that it would be some Motown soul, his favourite music to wash dishes to. Donuts and Discs was essentially a marriage of Pete's two favourite things – food and music.

"OK, Dad." Hope looked back at the girl. "Sorry, were you going to say something?"

But she shook her head. "Nah, it doesn't matter. I'll get out of your way."

* * *

Jazz trudged up the steps from the lagoon onto the seafront. Well, that had been a disaster. Ever since they'd got back from London, she'd been on a mission to try and meet someone – anyone – her age. Today she'd trawled around the shops in town, hanging out in all the sportswear shops she could find, hoping to spot a kindred spirit the way Amber had found her friend Sky at a vintage store. Jazz had seen a couple of girls who looked like fun rifling through some dance gear, and she'd followed them for a bit, but she chickened out of saying anything to them. What could she say without looking like a weirdo? And there was no way she was going to try and slip a Moonlight Dreamers postcard into their bags, as Amber had done. She'd probably get arrested! Then a security guard had started hovering near by and she realized she was probably giving off some serious shoplifter vibes.

She had walked home along the seafront feeling embarrassed and frustrated but then she'd spotted the girl outside the café. She'd been so close to trying to make conversation, it was just her luck that they were closing. Still, at least she had the consolation of a couple of delicious-looking doughnuts.

Jazz walked past the row of candy-coloured beach huts until she reached the end of the seafront and the sign saying PRIVATE that led to her road. The road contained twelve houses, all backing onto the sea, and all with their own private beach. Apparently her street was *the* place to live in

Brighton, and had been home to various celebrities over the years. The houses were nothing special to look at from the front, just a row of nondescript white boxes, really. Inside, it was a whole other story. The huge windows lining the rear of each house framed stunning and ever-changing views of the ocean. Even in her unhappy state, Jazz couldn't find fault with the view. Back in Australia the beach had been a couple of minutes' walk away, but this place was like living on a boat, especially when the tide came in, licking and frothing at the decking.

As she drew closer to her house at the end of the road, a dog came bolting out from the house next door, dragging a petite olive-skinned girl dressed all in black with cropped brown hair.

"Reggie, slow down!" the girl yelled, then, as she raced past Jazz, "Sorry, someone's dying to get out!"

Jazz smiled. According to her parents, the house next door belonged to an ageing star from a British soap opera. Perhaps this girl was her granddaughter? She looked about the same age as Jazz, who felt a prickle of hope. What if this girl came to visit her grandmother regularly? Or, even better, what if she lived with her? Maybe they could become friends…

Portia unclipped Reggie's lead and watched as he scampered off to the sea's edge, his head raised, barking and yelping at a hovering seagull. Even though Reggie had the crinkly face, stubby nose and square muzzle of a pug she could have sworn that he was a bird trapped inside a dog's body, the way he always leapt up, trying and failing to join the gulls.

Or maybe he was just crazy.

People did say that dogs became just like their owners and Reggie's owner, Shirley, was eccentric to say the least. Perhaps it was because she was an actor – a soap opera actor at that – but Shirley had a knack of turning every little thing into a drama. Like the time a traffic warden gave her a ticket (for parking totally illegally on the pavement outside her hairdresser because she didn't want to get rain on her perm) and she'd threatened to take him to the European Court of Human Rights. Or the time a pair of Jehovah's Witnesses had called at her house to discuss the rapidly approaching end of the world and she'd attempted to put them under citizen's arrest for "disturbing her peace of mind".

Even just now, when Portia had turned up to walk Reggie, Shirley had informed her that a "problem child" had moved in next door. "All I've heard are tantrums and slamming doors," she'd said, pursing her brightly painted lips. "It'll be drugs and sex next, you mark my words."

Portia wondered if the blonde girl she'd just passed was Shirley's new neighbour. She didn't look like a problem child about to start a drugs and sex binge; she looked more like an athlete in her tracksuit, her skin glowing with health. Facts wouldn't stop Shirley from having a good gossip, though.

A strong wind was whipping in from the sea causing the waves to crash and froth, and Portia's eyes to water, but she didn't mind. She found the sea so much more exciting and mysterious when it got lively. She was one of the few people who actually preferred the beach in winter, when the cold winds stripped Brighton of its tourists and holiday-makers, and only the hardiest locals took a stroll along the front. She smiled as another seagull swooped in, causing Reggie to practically hyperventilate with excitement.

Turning her face to the wind, Portia breathed in the salty air. Tomorrow was the first day of the new school year. After six weeks at home with her three crazy brothers and equally noisy parents she was kind of looking forward to the relative peace and tranquillity of a city secondary school.

And didn't *that* say everything anyone needed to know about her home life? She'd barely seen any of the kids she hung out with in school over the holidays and she felt a slight nervousness at the thought of having to reconnect. It wasn't that she didn't like her fellow classmates, it was more that she didn't really have much in common with them. To Portia, being in school felt a bit like accidentally ending up at a party you haven't been invited to — full of awkward conversations and stilted attempts to break the ice.

Reggie finally gave up trying to fly and scampered back over, tail wagging and fur dripping with sea spray. Portia crouched down and petted him as he licked her face. She sighed. If only humans could be as straightforward as dogs.

Chapter Five

"Mum! How much longer are you going to be?" Allegra banged on the bathroom door in frustration.

"I'm doing a deep conditioner on my hair, honey," Magdalena replied over the jaunty beats of breakfast radio.

"Oh my god! I've got to get to school. You're going to make me late on my first day back." Allegra slumped against the wall. Truth was, she'd happily stay in bed and not go to school at all, especially after the weirdness of what had happened at the weekend with Alf, but sadly that was not an option. "Come on!" she yelled, raising her fist to bang on the door again.

"All right, all right…" The door burst open and Magdalena came out in a cloud of coconut-scented steam, one towel wrapped round her head and another round her body.

"Be quick," she snapped, her Spanish accent thickening as it always did when she was annoyed. "I have work too."

You work in a hair salon, Allegra wanted to respond. *Surely you could spend all the time in the world on your hair there?* But she was running too late for any more bickering. After slamming the bathroom door behind her, Allegra wiped a clean patch in the steamy mirror and inspected her reflection. It was too late to wash her hair – there was so much of it she'd never get it dry in time. She'd have to put it up instead. After tying it back in a high ponytail she cleansed her face and took a quick shower then let out a wail at the sight of the empty towel rail.

"Muuuuuuum!"

Ten minutes later, Allegra was marching her way down the road to the bus stop, PE kit slung over one shoulder, her school bag heavy with books over the other. To Allegra, carrying so many books was its own pointless form of torture: there wasn't a single subject at school that she even came close to enjoying – apart from PE, but that was only when they were doing cross-country. (And that didn't require a single book!) Running gave her the chance to burn off some of her frustration. Sometimes she'd pretend she was running through the landscapes she longed to be adventuring in, like the mountainous region of Spain where her abuela lived, or the grid-like streets of New York, or the Amazonian rainforests. The world was so full of awesome places waiting to be discovered that it felt like a crime that she should have to remain trapped inside a classroom.

The bus stop was empty when she reached it and she breathed a sigh of relief. The one bonus of having a bathroom-hogging mother was that it meant she was late and had missed her friends, and them quizzing her about what had happened on her date with Alf – or rather what *hadn't* happened. She plonked her bags down on the floor. Why did life have to be so confusing?

She spotted the familiar flash of burgundy as someone in school uniform made their way towards the bus stop through the drizzle and her heart sank. What if it was one of her friends, ready to give her an inquisition? A sudden gust of wind whipped their umbrella to the side and she caught a glimpse of bright auburn hair and deathly pale skin. It was only the girl whose parents owned the café down at the lagoon. Even though they were in the same year at school – and in a couple of the same classes – Allegra had never spoken to her. It wasn't that she had anything against the girl; it was just that they didn't move in the same circles. Allegra hung with the crowd who, if they'd been in America, would have been the jocks and the cheerleaders. The girl from the café – Hope? – hung with… Allegra frowned. She didn't actually know. Hope reached the bus shelter and put down her umbrella, but as soon as she saw Allegra, she turned away.

Fine, be like that, Allegra thought. A bus appeared through the misty rain, brakes hissing like a balloon deflating as it pulled up alongside them.

Jazz sank further into the passenger seat, wishing she had the power to shrink to nothing as her dad parked outside the entrance to Cedars College. With its ornate architecture and tree-lined driveway, this place was worlds apart from the basic modern buildings of her old state school.

"There you go, darlin'." Mikey turned down the Pink Floyd track blaring from the stereo and grinned.

"Thanks," Jazz muttered.

"You got everything?"

"Yep."

"Don't worry, you're gonna ace it."

Easy for you to say, she wanted to snap. He could drop her there and go off to do something he loved. He wasn't the one who had to spend the day trying to fit in with hundreds of strangers, feeling like a jigsaw piece that had fallen into the wrong box.

He put his hand on her arm and gave her a warm smile. "You'll be fine. They're gonna love you."

Her dad being nice wasn't making it any easier. In fact, it was making her want to throw herself into his arms and sob.

"Thanks." She pulled away and unclipped her seatbelt, then opened the door, her fear increasing with every thud of her heart. "See you later."

"Have a great day," Mikey said, turning the music back up.

Jazz got out of the car and shut the door. Now there was no going back. Other students all wearing the same black-and-white uniform streamed past her, as slick and shiny as penguins. She quickly did up the top button on her shirt, took her phone from her pocket and looked at the message her best friend, Lisa, had sent her.

Don't let those stuck-up Poms get you down. I love you!
xxxx

Jazz followed the crowd through the school gates. She'd been told to report to the office. As she made her way into the reception area, she watched the hordes of students milling along the corridor. The noise was deafening, with everyone greeting one another like long-lost friends, which, of course, they were. Jazz's mouth went dry.

Finally, the woman behind the counter beckoned Jazz over. Jazz gave her name and year number and the woman told her to take a seat and said that someone would be there to get her shortly. When a buzzer started bleeping from speakers in the ceiling, the hordes thinned and the noise subsided. Jazz swallowed hard and took a deep breath. A girl with dark hair and thick glasses hurried along the corridor towards reception, glancing at Jazz with a quick smile, before going over to the desk. Jazz heard her full name – Jasmine – and she looked longingly at the door, wishing she could flee. But the girl was now heading her way, smiling broadly.

"Hi, I'm Bethany," she said. "I've come to take you to your form room."

Jasmine picked up her bag. "I'm Jazz," she replied, her dry mouth making her voice crack.

They walked this way and that along gleaming wood-panelled corridors without saying a word. Jazz felt panic rising inside her: there was no way she'd be able to remember her way out of this labyrinth. Finally, they stopped beside a closed door.

"Well, this is it," Bethany said, raising her eyebrows as if to say, *Good luck – you're gonna need it.* She opened the door and Jazz followed her inside.

An elderly man with wiry grey hair and round glasses sat behind a polished wooden desk at the front of the class, with about twenty students sitting in neat rows before him. All of them turned to stare at Jazz.

The teacher peered over his glasses at her. "Aha. Jasmine, I assume," he said in the poshest accent Jazz had ever heard.

"Yes," Jazz replied, her voice coming out like a squeak.

"Jasmine has come all the way from the Antipodes," he announced to the rest of the class theatrically. "Please, take a seat." He pointed to an empty desk in the middle of the room.

Jazz made her way to the desk, her face burning.

"Let's introduce ourselves, shall we?" the teacher said.

"Oh yes. G'day, I'm Jazz," she murmured.

"Actually, I meant we should introduce ourselves to you," he said, causing Jazz to blush even more. "I'm Mr Montague." He then gestured to the girl at the front of the class.

"I'm Annabelle," she said in a voice so clipped and polished she sounded like royalty.

One by one the students introduced themselves but to Jazz it was like white noise, their words drowned out by her stressed thoughts. She'd never felt so different before, and so out of place. It was set to be a *very* long day.

Hope handed the doctor's letter to Ms Sykes and watched the PE teacher's smile fade while her eyes scanned the page.

"Oh, Hope," she said, as she read. "I'm so sorry to hear this."

Hope became aware of a slight hush among the girls closest to them in the changing room. Although she couldn't bring herself to look at them, she could feel the heat of their stares.

"When did this happen? When were you diagnosed?" Ms Sykes stopped reading and looked at Hope, her face full of sympathy.

"At the start of the summer holidays," Hope said quietly. The one good thing about being diagnosed with hypertrophic cardiomyopathy at the start of the holiday was that she hadn't had to tell many people about it. Now she was back at school, the reality of her condition – and the changes it was going to make to her life – was becoming all too apparent.

"That must have been very frightening," Ms Sykes said. The silence around them grew as more of the girls tuned in to their conversation.

"It's OK," Hope feigned nonchalance. "My mum has HCM too and it can be hereditary, so we always knew there was a chance I might get it." A fifty per cent chance to be exact. Hope had been the daughter to draw the short straw – or the thickened wall in her heart, to be more specific.

Ms Sykes glanced back at the letter. "It says here that you can still do moderate exercise?"

Hope nodded. One of the many unfair things about her diagnosis was that it had the greatest impact on her favourite subject, with her favourite teacher. Why couldn't she have inherited a condition that made her at risk from physics, or algebra?

"How do you feel about trying some netball?" Ms Sykes continued. "You could be goalkeeper, less running."

"OK." Hope's face smarted as she noticed Allegra Lopez staring at her. Goalkeeper was normally Allegra's position since she was about seven feet tall, with legs that seemed to go on for ever. Hope offered her a feeble smile but Allegra had already turned away, muttering something unintelligible to her friends.

They all filed outside, where a drizzly mist hung in the air. It was only September but it already felt as cold as winter. Hope shivered and hugged her arms to herself. *You can do this, you're not going to die*, she thought as she walked onto the court and took up her position. *You're allowed to do moderate exercise.* She felt an ominous fluttering in her chest. *Deep breaths*, she said silently, remembering the advice her mum had given her. Ever since Hope's diagnosis, her mum had offered endless tips on how to make living with HCM more manageable. Hope couldn't help wondering if this was partly out of guilt as well as a desire to help – she had been the one to give Hope HCM after all. *Stop thinking that!* she scolded herself. *It isn't Mum's fault.* She took a deep breath. Ms Sykes blew her whistle and the game began.

At first, all went well, as Hope's team had the majority of the possession and the ball hardly came near her end of the court. But then, suddenly, the tide turned and a swarm of girls in bright red bibs began bearing down on her. Once this would have got Hope's heart racing for all the right reasons and she'd have thrown herself into her role as defender, but now fear rooted her to the spot. What if one of them charged into her? What if she got an elbow to her chest? She knew she wasn't thinking straight; there was no way this game, however vigorous, would hurt her heart, but she couldn't get calm. The other side's goal attack threw the ball high. Allegra leapt up but it soared over her outstretched arms, straight into the hands of the other team's goal shooter, Chantelle.

"Block it!" Allegra yelled.

Chantelle took aim. Hope knew she needed to leap but she remained frozen. The ball swooped up in a perfect arc and slid through the net. As the other team hugged and cheered, Hope heard Allegra say, "Shit!" She felt terrible. She hated letting her side down. Before she could stop it her eyes filled with tears. Turning so the others wouldn't see, she wiped her eyes with the back of her hand. But it was as if all the sorrow that had been building since her diagnosis had been unleashed and, no matter how hard she tried, she couldn't contain it any more. This was how her life was going to be from now on.

"Hope!" She heard someone yell her name and turned to see a blur of red through her tears. The other team were descending on her again.

"What are you doing?" Allegra yelled as Chantelle raced past Hope and scored again.

"I'm sorry — I…"

Ms Sykes came running over. "Do you want me to sub you?"

"Yes please," Hope whispered.

Ms Sykes blew her whistle and beckoned the substitute onto the court. "Go and take a seat and watch," she said to Hope.

Hope trudged over to the bench. Yes, this was how her life was going to be from now on: she'd be an onlooker confined to the sidelines while everyone else raced by, leaving her behind — even Megan, her one true friend, and the sibling who had drawn the long straw in the genetic lottery.

As Portia sat at the back of her History class observing the behaviour of her classmates, it reminded her of the nature documentaries she loved. *And if you watch very closely, you will observe the mating ritual of the spotted teenage boy*, she said voice-over-style in her head, as she noticed a kid named David Green flick a ball of chewed-up paper at the back of Amy Jones's head. She picked up her pen and started doodling a cartoon image of David at the back of her exercise book, all gangly limbs and a chin pockmarked with acne.

"Hey!" Amy cried, smoothing down her immaculately groomed hair with her immaculately manicured hand.

You will notice that the female of the teenage species spends an inordinate amount of time preening, Portia's private voice-over continued as she began doodling Amy leaning her head on an ironing board. *Rumour has it, they even iron their hair straight!*

She sighed. She'd only been back in school for a few hours and already boredom was creeping over her. As much as her brothers had got on her nerves at times during the summer holiday, at least she'd been free to do what she pleased. She'd been able to lose herself in the exciting tales from her favourite graphic novels – she'd even started work on a graphic novel of her own – and she'd been able to hang out with her beloved four-legged friends. Portia had first thought of launching her own dog-walking business after her parents told her there was no way they would get her a dog of her own. "It's enough of a menagerie with four kids," her dad had laughed when she'd asked. But Portia had been blessed with an indomitable spirit – or, as her parents preferred to say, she was as stubborn as a mule – and so she'd come up with the idea for "Pooch Patrol – Dog-Walking Service to the Stars".

The subheading had been Shirley's idea. She'd been the first person to respond to Portia's advert on the noticeboard at her local newsagent. Due to the long hours Shirley spent filming in London, she needed someone to take Reggie out most mornings and evenings. Portia had begun walking him at the start of the summer holidays and he was her favourite.

When her parents told her she could keep only one client once she went back to school, it had been a no-brainer – Portia's heart belonged to the wannabe seagull, Reggie. Her parents had also said that she could only keep walking him as long as her grades didn't slip. She stopped doodling and focused on her teacher. She'd better start paying attention.

Chapter Six

Jazz lay on her bed and sighed. She got up and stood at her window and sighed. She looked at the time on her phone and sighed. She wondered if it was possible to pass out from lack of oxygen due to too much sighing – and sighed. It was nine o'clock on Saturday morning. Normally by this time, she'd have been surfing for a couple of hours and she and her friends would be dragging their boards over the warm sand to the local café for a stack of fluffy pancakes with eggs and bacon. The hunger she got from surfing was like no other and made everything taste extra delicious, but now she seemed to have lost her appetite completely. She looked at her phone and sighed again. Then she sent a quick message to Lisa.

**Hey. What's happening? How's your Saturday going?
xxxx**

She stared at the screen, willing Lisa to reply. It was early evening in Australia. She was probably out having fun. A terrible thought occurred to Jazz. What if Lisa was already forgetting about her? What if she'd already found a new best friend? A notification chimed on her phone and relief surged through her. But it wasn't a message from Lisa; it was from Amber.

> Bonjour from Paris! Just wondering how your first week at school has been? Xx

Jazz sat on her bed and started typing a reply.

> Great! Loving it so far...

She stopped mid-message. It didn't feel right lying to her cousin but, equally, she didn't want to look pitiful either. She deleted what she'd typed and started again.

> OK, I guess. How about you? How's it going in Paris? Xx

A few moments later a reply arrived.

> I thought my French was OK until I came to live here. They all speak so fast I can't keep up! Don't forget to play What Would Oscar Say? ☺ xx

The first week at school had been so stressful and all-consuming that Jazz had totally forgotten about the book Amber had given her. She reached into the top drawer of her bedside cabinet and took out the velvet bag. "All right, Oscar, how the hell am I supposed to enjoy yet another weekend with no friends?" she whispered, before flicking the book open to a random page.

"*I always like to know everything about my new friends, and nothing about my old ones*" the quote read.

"What the…?" Jazz stared at the page. It had to be a coincidence that the page she had landed upon contained a quote about friends. Didn't it? Her phone pinged again.

Well, did you play it yet? What did he say? Xx

Jazz typed up the quote and sent it to Amber. As she studied the words, she had mixed feelings. She couldn't imagine never wanting to know anything about her old friends. They were all she could think about right now. But maybe that was the problem…

Oh wow, I needed to hear that one too xx

Came the reply from Amber. And then another message popped on to the screen:

I don't suppose you've made any postcards to give out yet?

Jazz shuddered at the thought. All week at school she'd felt like a freak just for talking differently to the others.

They were all so well spoken, with their sharp consonants and polished vowels, it made her even more self-conscious of her Australian accent. If she started handing out random postcards, she'd be cast as the resident weirdo for sure.

Not yet xx

But Amber wasn't giving up.

I dare you to give out a couple this weekend. I'm going to go and hang out in a café to see if I can find myself a new friend. Oscar's inspired me. It's so much fun getting to know new people. Good luck on your search too! xx

Jazz replied, **Thank you! xx**, then she emptied the remaining contents of the velvet bag onto her bed. As well as the book, the set of rules and the dog-eared postcard, a beautiful gemstone fell out that glowed blueish-white, like the moon. Jazz picked up the stone and popped it on her nightstand then she looked at the postcard. Maybe part of the problem was that it was too much in Amber's voice. She gazed out of the window at the iron-grey sea. What would she say if she were trying to find some like-minded friends? She opened the note app on her phone and started typing:

Do you ever feel like there must be more to life than fitting in? Are you proud to be different? Would you like to meet other free-spirited people? Do you love the sea?

She looked back at Amber's postcard. She liked the idea of asking people to talk about a quote as a way of getting in touch, but maybe she could change it a little. She leafed back through the book of quotes until she found the one she wanted. Then she fetched a paper bag full of postcards she'd bought in town the previous weekend. They featured photos of Brighton sights and she'd been thinking of sending them to her friends back home with WISH YOU WERE HERE! written in bold. But maybe she could use them to try and find a new friend outside of school? It wasn't as if she had anything to lose. She took a card from the bag and began to write.

As Allegra watched Alf kick the ball across the beach to his friend Danny, a strange, numb feeling grew inside her. It was weird. For the whole of the last school year – including holidays, weekends and inset days – she'd pined for Alf and his footballer's legs and dark wavy hair and dimples. If a scientist had been monitoring her brain activity, they would have recorded entire weeks' worth of daydreams in which Allegra and Alf were an item. But now she was actually living inside one of those dreams – hanging out on the beach with him on a Saturday – she couldn't help feeling a crushing sense of disappointment. It was a bit like the year she'd longed for a Barbie house. She'd finally got one for Christmas but the shine had worn off by Boxing Day – it hadn't been nearly as good as it looked in the adverts.

Danny kicked the ball back to Alf, who stopped it with ease. He was one of the best footballers in his year, which instantly made him popular with both the boys and girls. Being Alf's girlfriend was like scooping first prize, so why did she feel so flat inside? Where had the tingles in the pit of her stomach gone? She thought back to the previous weekend when, after a summer of flirting, he'd finally asked her out. They'd gone for a walk to the lagoon where they sat and drank milkshakes outside the café. It was the first time it had been just the two of them and, left to their own conversational devices, Allegra had made a worrying discovery: without his friends to banter with, Alf didn't really have a lot to say. When she'd asked him where he'd like to travel, he'd shrugged and said, "I wouldn't mind going on a lads' holiday to Magaluf." And when she'd asked him what he wanted to do when he left school – a question which dominated most of her waking thoughts – he'd looked at her blankly, then muttered that he didn't really care. And then, when he'd tried to kiss her, she'd pulled away as if she'd been burned. His mouth had felt so awkward on hers, his tongue prodding and flicking like a lizard's; it was nothing like the passionate embrace she'd fantasized about.

Alf did a fancy trick with the ball and returned it to Danny, grinning at Allegra.

"Great kick," she called, staring out at the sea beyond him. She loved how every day it was a different colour. Today, it was as grey as pencil lead, reflecting the clouds above, apart from the tips of the waves, which frothed white. She breathed in the salty air and instantly felt better. She'd opted to hang out with Alf today because Chantelle and her other girl friends were going clothes shopping. Allegra hated clothes shopping, especially on a Saturday. The big-name stores her friends shopped at felt chaotic at the weekend and never seemed to sell anything different or interesting. At least here she could breathe and watch the sea. She looked out across the water and thought of France over the horizon and beyond it the rest of Europe. *There's a whole world out there*, she reassured herself. *Things won't stay like this for ever.*

Portia let herself into Shirley's house and prepared for the furry cyclone that was Reggie to hit. Yelping excitedly, he came barrelling down the hallway towards her.

"Hello, Reggie, I'm very happy to see you too," she laughed, crouching down and scratching him behind the ears, breathing in his doggy smell. Once he'd covered her face in kisses she clipped his lead to his collar and took him outside. Almost as soon as they'd got down the front steps, Reggie squatted. Portia put her backpack on the floor and took a floral-scented bag from the front pocket. Having to scoop poop was the only drawback of being a dog-lover but it was a price she was willing to pay – even today, when it took several attempts to scrape it off the pavement. As she stood up, Reggie began barking excitedly at something behind her. She turned to see the "problem child" from next door standing by her backpack.

"Oh, hey, sorry," Portia said, glancing at the poop bag with an apologetic smile.

"No worries," the girl replied before hurrying past.

According to Shirley's latest update, the girl's dad was some kind of hotshot music producer. "The whole family are probably on drugs," she'd said in an ominous stage whisper. "You know what those music industry folk are like, they just don't take their craft seriously like us actors do, they see it as one big excuse for a party."

Portia had nodded, even though she had zero clue about music industry folk and what they got up to. She watched the girl break into a sprint towards the seafront. Well, if she was a delinquent she was certainly a very fit one!

Jazz ran and ran until the pain in her lungs burned the embarrassment away. She couldn't believe she'd done it: she'd delivered one of her postcards. While the girl was distracted cleaning up after her dog, she'd felt the sudden compulsion to take one of the cards from her pocket and shove it inside the discarded backpack. At least now she'd have something to report back to Amber when she next checked in, Jazz tried to reassure herself. And besides, there was no way the girl could prove the card had come from her.

Her mind began to calm and she slowed her pace slightly, looking out across the sea. As Jazz ran further, she began to feel a strange sense of elation. At least she'd done something, at least she'd tried to change her situation for the better. She ran as far as the i360, a strange tower-like structure with a ring-shaped platform that travelled up and down all day, treating visitors to panoramic views of the city and the sea.

After pausing to catch her breath, she began jogging back. When she reached the lagoon, she turned and went down the steps. The pink neon sign for Donuts and Discs blinked invitingly against the grey of the sky. Jazz hadn't had any breakfast apart from an apple, and the thought of one of those doughnuts was making her drool.

As soon as she stepped inside, the warmth of the café wrapped itself around her. A funky disco track was playing – on vinyl, judging by the crackles coming through the speakers – and the air smelled of warm sugar and cinnamon. There was no sign of the girl from last time. Jazz ordered a cappuccino and a mocha doughnut from a red-haired woman behind the counter, and took them to a table in the corner by a window.

As she sipped her coffee, she looked out across the lagoon at the people hurrying along the footpath, dressed warmly against the cold. It was all so dreary compared to home, like looking at the world through a washed-out filter. It was so uninspiring she hadn't taken a photo for Instagram for weeks and she hadn't even dared look at her social feeds to see what her friends were up to, the FOMO was way too strong.

Jazz was just finishing her doughnut when a door behind the counter opened and the girl with the red hair came out and started clearing a table. Jazz felt the same compulsion she'd felt earlier, a reckless sense of having nothing to lose. She swigged down the last of her coffee, then tucked one of her postcards beneath her plate before hurrying for the door.

Hope looked out of the steamy window as some seagulls took flight from the roof of the boat shed on the other side of the lagoon. *Oh, to be able to fly off whenever and wherever you want*, she thought wistfully.

She went over to the next table and picked up a cup streaked with the remnants of a cappuccino. As she picked up the plate next to it, she saw a postcard sticking out. It was a picture of Brighton Palace Pier – far less interesting than the West Pier, in Hope's humble opinion, which had been destroyed in a fire back in 2003. Its skeletal remains still stood in the sea, like something out of a Gothic horror story. As she put the card on her tray to throw it away, she noticed that someone had written something on the back. She turned it over.

ARE YOU A MOONLIGHT DREAMER?

- Do you ever feel like there must be more to life than fitting in?

- Are you proud to be different?

- Would you like to meet other free-spirited people?

- Do you love the sea?

When you read this quote, what does it mean to you? "We are all in the gutter, but some of us are looking at the stars."

Email your answer to: jazzed@googlepost.com

Hope stared at the card. There was no stamp or address on it so clearly it hadn't been intended to be posted, but what or who was it intended for? She glanced out of the window. It was still early and the weather was pretty grim so there were only a couple of dog walkers and a jogger in sight. Had whoever was sitting at this table left it here on purpose?

She reread the text, this time mentally answering yes to each of the questions. Then she read the quote. What did it mean to her? Hope frowned. Was it true that everyone was in the gutter? Surely some people had it a lot easier than others. She watched as one of the joggers raced by and felt a pang of yearning. Not everyone had a heart condition for a start. *Don't think about it. . .*

She shoved the postcard into her apron pocket and took the dirty dishes into the kitchen.

Chapter Seven

Portia lay on her bed and stared up at the ceiling. She'd recently read a post about how to maintain a sense of calm in the midst of chaos and the writer had said that even noise can be soothing if you listen to it mindfully. "*Be aware of the sounds you're hearing without judgement,*" she'd written.

Hmm.

Portia closed her eyes. From outside she could hear the incessant hum of traffic, then the beep of a car horn. The piercing shriek of a seagull rose above the faint bassline of a car stereo – or maybe it was coming from the pub across the road. Some men were singing – it was Saturday, so it was probably a football song. Inside the house the faint tuneless plonking of one of her mum, Amanda's, piano students drifted up from the living room. She could hear the deep drone of her dad Kamran's voice in his study, and the explosions from her older brother Darius's Xbox in his bedroom next door. Darius hadn't been allowed a war game until he turned sixteen as their parents thought it might "encourage violent tendencies". Now it was all he played, going on endless killing sprees as if he was making up for lost time. He never wanted to play *Minecraft* with Portia any more. She frowned. How could she not hear the twins? She could always hear Casper and Arsham – unless they were asleep. Then she heard a crash, followed by a yelp, followed by peals of laughter.

Portia sat up. There was no way you could feel calm in this house. She'd bet that even the most enlightened Buddhist monk would be pushed to the brink of a nervous breakdown after a day inside these walls. Even the super calm and steely hero of the graphic novel she was working on, Labradora, would lose it here, surrounded by Portia's brothers. She looked at her backpack, lying on the floor as menacingly as an IED. (Portia now knew all about improvised explosive devices, thanks to Darius's obsession with *Call of Duty*.) Ticking away inside her bag was her French homework.

She normally liked to get her homework done as quickly as possible so she could get back to working on the illustrations for her novel but, no matter how hard she tried, she just couldn't get to grips with French. Why did they have to give a gender to everything, even inanimate objects? Like, why should a chair be masculine or feminine? It didn't make any sense and it just created unnecessary stress.

Portia stared longingly at the doors of her fitted wardrobe, which had become a giant vision board for her novel. One of the doors was covered with scene cards containing plot ideas and the other was full of rough pencil sketches of her characters. She could practically hear them calling to her, pleading to be fleshed out and coloured in.

"You do realize your bedroom's starting to look like a murderer's lair," Darius had said to her the last time she granted him permission to enter. "They always stick pictures of their victims all over their walls."

"They aren't victims, they're characters," Portia had tried to explain, but Darius had just grunted and shrugged and sloped back to his stinky pit with its posters of soldiers and weapons plastered all over the walls. Clearly her brother didn't do irony.

With a heavy sigh, Portia picked up her backpack. The sooner she started, the sooner it would be over. As she pulled out her French folder, a postcard fluttered to the floor. She picked it up, trying to work out where it might have come from. On one side there was a picture of the Royal Pavilion – or "the poor man's Taj Mahal" as her mum called it – and on the other was some writing. She began reading it out loud.

"'*Do you ever feel like there must be more to life than fitting in?*' Oh yes," she agreed enthusiastically. "'*Are you proud to be different?*' Hmm, I guess so. '*Would you like to meet other free-spirited people?*' Yup, if they exist. '*Do you love the sea?*' Absolutely! '*When you read this quote, what does it mean to you. . .*'" Portia studied the quote. It sounded vaguely familiar but she wasn't sure why or where she knew it from. Perhaps her English professor dad would know? She jotted the quote on a scrap of paper and went downstairs.

From the living room she could hear her mum's piano student attempting to play "Perfect" by Ed Sheeran. Portia winced as they hit yet another wrong note. Clearly they didn't do irony either. She opened the door to her dad's study to find him sitting at his desk with the twins. The board game Snakes and Ladders was set up in front of them.

"Good afternoon, daughter of mine," her dad greeted her with a warm smile. "Would you care to join us?"

"Good afternoon, father of mine. Sorry, I can't – French homework." She gave a helpless shrug, grateful for the first time ever for the verbs waiting to be conjugated up in her room. The twins were notorious cheats and playing board games with them could be so annoying.

"Sucks to be you." Casper grinned up at her as he shook the dice.

"Yeah," Arsham giggled.

"Yeah well, at least I'm not named after a friendly ghost," Portia replied, causing Arsham to snort with laughter.

"I'm not!" Casper yelled. "Dad, tell her. My name means bringer of treasure."

"Whatever." She smirked.

"Now, now, azizam," her dad chuckled. "You know your names are all a tribute to your Persian heritage, and none of you are named after a cartoon ghost."

"Thank you." Casper glared at Portia. She grinned back at him. She knew full well that her dad, who had moved to the UK from Iran as a child, had given them Persian names, but it was just *so* satisfying getting her own back on her brothers.

"Dad, do you know where this quote is from?" Portia put the piece of paper in front of him.

"Of course," he replied instantly. "It's Oscar Wilde." He glanced at the book-lined walls of the study. "I have several of his books and plays if you'd like to borrow them."

"It's OK, that's all I needed, thank you."

Once Portia was back in her bedroom she studied the quote, trying to figure out what it meant to her. *Surely it means that we all have the choice to look on the bright side*, she thought to herself. Should she respond to the card though? She'd answered yes to all of the questions and although she wasn't exactly sure what a Moonlight Dreamer was, she liked the sound of it. She had no clue how the card had found its way into her bag but it was way more fun than her French homework. She clicked on her email app and began writing a new message.

Dear Mystery Postcard Sender,

I think I might be a Moonlight Dreamer as I answered yes to all of your questions. Unless of course it's a trick and we're supposed to answer no. Anyway, I'm not sure how you got your card in my bag but I do love a good mystery and I love a good quote too. To me, Oscar Wilde's saying that although life can be crap for all of us, some of us are able to look on the bright side. I would definitely class myself as one of those people. But enough about me, who are you? And how did you get a postcard in my bag without me realizing?!

P

She reread the email, making sure that she hadn't given too much away, and pressed SEND.

Hope sat at one of the tables outside the café and took a breath. It was late afternoon, the lunchtime rush was finally over and she was on her break. After being missing in action for the entire day, the sun was peeping cautiously through the banks of cloud, bathing the lagoon in a pale glow. She sipped on her hot chocolate with a shot of caramel and took the postcard from her pocket. It had been filling her mind with questions all afternoon, and she felt compelled to respond. It had been great having something else to think about while she worked – something that wasn't related to the Great Unmentionable going on inside her body. She opened up a new email and began to write.

I'm not exactly sure who you are and what this is all about but I found your postcard today at the café and... She paused. What should she write next? *And my life is so tragic I have nothing better to do than reply to a random postcard that, for all I know, could be some kind of prank...* But there was something about the postcard, something about the words that made her feel certain the sentiment behind them was genuine. She continued writing... *I definitely answered yes to all of the questions. I wasn't sure about the quote, though. I don't think it's true that we're all in the gutter. Some people seem to have no problems in life...*

As if on cue, she noticed Allegra and some boys from her school strolling down the steps from the seafront into the lagoon. *Some people are popular and pretty and have loads of friends and not a care in the world, whereas other people have loads of crap to deal with. Like life-changing health conditions that make everything so much harder.* She took another breath, she wasn't supposed to be thinking about that any more, let alone writing about it to a complete stranger, but now she'd started she couldn't seem to stop. *I was diagnosed with a heart condition this summer, so I would say that my life is definitely in the gutter right now, and yes, I suppose I'm still able to see the stars but in a way that just makes me feel worse, because it reminds me of everything I've lost.* She paused again. Her response had become way more negative than she'd intended. But did it really matter? She didn't have a clue who she was writing to. And they didn't have a clue who she was, so she might as well use the opportunity to offload. *So yes, I definitely feel like there's more to life than fitting in because now I'll never fit in, not truly.*

Hope (Oh, the irony!)

The air filled with chatter and laughter as Allegra and her friends drew closer. Hope quickly pressed SEND and stood up.

"Hey, don't you go to Hove Secondary?" a boy named Alf called over, spinning a football on his finger. Even though he was in the year above she knew his name. Everyone knew his name. He was captain of the football team, which automatically made him King of the World.

"Yeah," Hope replied. Much to her annoyance she could feel her face burning.

"And your parents own this place, right?"

"Yes."

"So, what are the chances of getting us some free doughnuts?"

"Leave it, Alf," Hope heard Allegra murmur.

"She's in your year, though, isn't she?" Alf said, turning to Allegra.

"Yeah, but…" Allegra looked at Hope. "We're not exactly friends."

"Why not?" Alf came over to Hope and she felt her pulse quicken. She found his arrogance as overbearing as the cheap aftershave he was wearing. "Don't you like my girlfriend?"

"I don't know her." Hope's voice came out a lot terser than she'd intended.

"All right, calm down." He was right in her face now, so close she could smell the minty chewing gum on his breath. "Moody bitch."

"Come on, let's go somewhere else," one of the other boys said. Hope turned away, her vision blurred from a mixture of anger and fear. Leaving what was left of her drink on the table she hurried inside.

Chapter Eight

As Allegra sat in the chip shop, she felt like she was stuck inside a world where all the settings had been distorted. Alf and his friends were way too loud, the smell of the fish frying was way too strong and the bright red of the Formica-topped tables made her eyes hurt. All she wanted was to be outside in the fresh air. Even though she and Hope weren't friends, she felt really bad about what had just happened. Seeing Alf talk to Hope like that had added yet another strike against him. But if he could be that forceful over something that didn't really matter what would he be like if she ended things with him? *Don't be so stupid*, she told herself sternly. *You can handle him.*

She took her phone from her bag, hoping for the first time in her life that her mum had messaged, asking her to come home. But Magdalena always went out after work on a Saturday with the girls from the salon, or on one of her internet dates. Allegra shuddered at the thought. At least Magdalena had agreed to stop bringing her dates back home, so there'd be no more pervy guys lurking in the living room.

She clicked on one of her old messages and pretended to read it.

"I've got to go," she said to Alf, who was busy trying to throw chips into Danny's open mouth.

"What? Why?" He turned to her and frowned. He might be cute when things were going his way but he wasn't quite so attractive when his eyes hardened and his dimples faded.

"My mum's asking me to come home. We're – we're having people over for dinner."

"Can't you tell her you've got plans?"

"Nah." Allegra shook her head. "She'd ground me."

Alf sighed.

Allegra stood up and put on her jacket. "See you later then."

"Yeah, all right," Alf replied moodily.

Ignoring his sulk, she made her way outside. A flock of starlings swooped by overhead, off to the pier to roost for the night. She watched as the cloud of birds soared together as one, with all the elegance of a perfectly choreographed dance troupe. There was something so soothing about the way they flew. The shop door opened and Alf came out and her heart sank. She really hoped he didn't want to walk her home.

"Don't I get a kiss goodbye?" he asked and the cheeky grin reappeared.

"Oh – yeah – sure."

He stepped towards her and put his hands on her shoulders. Then his mouth clamped down on top of hers.

For so long she'd dreamt of kissing Alf. For so long she'd *practised* kissing Alf on her pillow. In her dreams, and on her pillow, he'd been passionate and tender. But in reality, he was awkward and forceful and, to make things even worse, his lips tasted of chip oil. Thankfully, after a couple of seconds, he let her go, glancing back over his shoulder into the shop, as if checking to see if his friends had noticed.

"All right, see you then," he said.

"Yes, see you." She wondered if he could sense her change of heart, if her doubts were as obvious as cartoon-style thought bubbles over her head. She hurried across the road, deciding to walk home along the seafront in the hope that it would clear her head. As she cut through the lagoon, she glanced over at Donuts and Discs. The neon sign outside was glowing bright pink against the darkening sky. She thought of Hope's face, and how stressed she'd looked when Alf had spoken to her. As much as Hope's stand-offishness annoyed her, Allegra felt really bad that Alf had frightened her, especially as there was a rumour going round that she'd been diagnosed with cancer over the holiday. Maybe Allegra could catch her now and say sorry.

She hurried around the lake to the café. The closed sign was hanging on the door and she could see a man who she guessed was Hope's dad clearing up behind the counter. There was no sign of Hope though. Allegra sighed. It would be a lot harder to try and make amends in school. As she went past the tables outside, she spotted a postcard sticking out from beneath a dirty cup. The words "free-spirited people" caught her eye. She paused and looked around. Apart from a lone dog walker on the other side of the lagoon there was no one in sight. She lifted the cup. The postcard had been handwritten but it didn't appear to be to anyone in particular. It was a bunch of questions, like one of those adverts asking if you'd been hurt in an accident that wasn't your fault. Only it wasn't plugging anything; it was just questions. Questions to which she was answering *yes* as she scanned the words. She quickly glanced around again then shoved the card in her pocket and hurried off to the seafront.

Jazz watched as Mikey expertly rolled a cigarette between his tanned fingers. "The thing about moving to a new country," he said, before licking the tissue-thin paper, "is that it's all about attitude. If you go in expecting the best, like I did all those years ago when I moved to Australia, you'll have the best time. If you go in expecting the worst, well…" He raised his eyebrows.

"I guess so," Jazz replied. It was the first time she'd agreed with him on anything since he'd announced that they were moving, and the momentousness of the occasion clearly hadn't been lost on him as his expression changed from surprise to delight within seconds. He lit his cigarette, leaned back on his seat and stared across the deck to the sea. The tide was out and a half-moon shone over the water. Even though it was freezing and they were both huddled beneath blankets, Jazz had to admit that it looked kind of cool. Ever since she'd received a reply to her postcard, she'd been on a weird high. She'd figured out that it was from the dog-walking girl next door; now she just had to figure out what to email back. Maybe she should ask Amber what she'd done when she got a response to her postcards. She took her phone from her pocket and saw that she had a new email notification. Surely it couldn't be… But it was. She'd got another response! Jazz grinned as she read the title: **We aren't all in the gutter.**

"Right, I'm going to get the barbie going," Mikey said, leaping to his feet. "What do you fancy? Hot dog? Burger? Chicken wings?"

"All of the above, please," Jazz replied, looking up from her phone.

"All righty then," he said, rubbing his hands together, clearly overjoyed. It was the first time she'd shown any enthusiasm for his food since they'd moved. "Your wish is my command, madam."

"Thank you, kind sir," Jazz replied, falling into their old-style banter. Much as she hated to admit it, it felt good to have called an emotional ceasefire. She opened the email and looked at the bottom. It was from someone called Hope and for some reason they'd written "Oh, the irony" in brackets after their name. She quickly began to read.

"Whoa!" she exclaimed as she reached the end. When she'd first seen the girl in the café, she'd assumed she had a great life, working in such a cool place, with awesome food and music on tap. But as one of her dad's most annoying sayings went, "Never assume – it makes an ass out of u and me." Jazz couldn't even begin to imagine what it must be like to live with a health condition, especially one that affected the heart. That was hardcore. For the first time since she'd gone into her monumental sulk about moving here, she felt something close to gratitude. At least she was still fit and healthy. At least one day she'd be able to return to Australia. She heard a sizzle from the other end of the deck as Mikey put some meat on the grill.

"Dad?" she called.

"Yes, honey."

"Love you."

He looked so surprised and grateful she almost started to cry.

"Love you more," he replied.

"Love you most," she called back. And – yet another first since she arrived in the UK – Jazz felt a warmth inside.

Allegra looked at the Post-it note stuck to the fridge door beneath a magnet from Barcelona. *Help yourself to ready meal, won't be too late*, Magdalena had written. Allegra opened the door and the cool white light bathed her face. In movies and TV shows, fridges always seemed to be heaving with food, but not theirs. Theirs was almost always a tragedy to fridge-kind and tonight was no exception. All it contained was a shepherd's pie ready meal, a tub of margarine and a little black pot containing Magdalena's "Youth Dew" face mask. If Magdalena put half as much effort into cooking as she did into beautifying herself, they would dine like queens, but sadly she seemed to have missed out on the cooking gene. It was really disappointing, as Magdalena's mother Sofia, Allegra's abuela, was renowned for making the best paella in all of Spain — or her home town in Spain, at least.

Allegra sighed. Maybe she should have stayed out with Alf. Even a plate of greasy chips would be better than an insipid shepherd's pie topped with watery potato. But then she'd have had to listen to him and his friends going on and on about football and who was the best at what and she'd have ended up wanting to squirt ketchup in her ears from the boredom.

Shutting the fridge, she remembered the postcard she'd found and took it from her pocket. This time she studied the quote at the bottom. *"We are all in the gutter, but some of us are looking at the stars."* She liked it. There was something hopeful about it and it reminded her of the many nights she would gaze out of her bedroom window at the sky — the one bonus of living at the top of a tower block was that the views were epic — and be reminded of the vastness of the universe. She loved the way her problems seemed to shrink down to a more manageable size after gazing at the stars. Perhaps she should write that in an email to the email address on the card. But what if it did turn out to be just an advert for something?

But what if it *wasn't*? Hadn't she been craving something exciting all summer long? She took out her phone, opened a new email and began to type.

Chapter Nine

After what she had to grudgingly admit was quite an enjoyable evening feasting on barbecued meat with her parents, Jazz made her way upstairs to bed. Of course, she wasn't actually going to bed yet; she had urgent Moonlight Dreamers business to attend to – a fact that filled her with happiness. She curled up against the pillows on her bed and opened Amber's latest message on her phone.

That's EPIC that you heard back from both girls!! Well done! When I got responses from Maali and Sky, I sent them an email thanking them for getting in touch and suggesting we meet at a local café. Maybe you could do the same? I think I just said they should come if they wanted to find out more about being a Moonlight Dreamer. I kept it really casual. Good luck and keep me posted! xx

Hmm, where should she suggest they meet? Donuts and Discs would have been perfect but it would be a bit weird to ask Hope to meet up there. She had to pick somewhere neutral, and public, so the girls would feel totally safe. They had no idea who they'd be meeting after all.

Jazz looked out of the window. It was so dark now she couldn't see the sea but she could still hear it, whispering back and forth on the pebbles. Maybe she should suggest they meet on the beach... Yes, that would be perfect, as long as the crappy British weather didn't ruin things. She looked up the forecast on her phone and saw to her surprise that there was a huge yellow sun forecast for tomorrow. But was tomorrow too soon? A Sunday would definitely be easier than a weekday and if she left it until next weekend they'd either have forgotten all about it, or be having second thoughts. She would probably be having second thoughts by then! Yes, sooner was definitely better.

She was about to start drafting an invite when her phone pinged. She had a new email. When Jazz saw that the title was **MOONLIGHT DREAMERS** her heart began to race. But it couldn't be another response to her postcards. She'd only given out two, and she'd received two replies – one from the girl with the backpack and one from the café. Maybe one of the girls had written to her again. She clicked the email open.

OK, I don't know if this is some kind of marketing thing but just in case it isn't... YES, I would like to meet other free-spirited people, and YES, I'm proud to be different, and YES, I love the sea. I really liked the quote too. It made me think of how I always feel better when I look up at the sky at night, and how the size of the universe

seems to make my problems shrink somehow. And I would totally
agree that we're all in the gutter and that school is the worst gutter
of all! I don't know what else to say, and I really hope this isn't a
prank. You have no idea how badly I need things to change!

"What the hell?" Jazz stared at the email, her skin tingling. Whoever had sent it hadn't signed it. She checked the email address: leggy_66@googlepost.com. It was totally different from the others. Somehow, a third person had seen one of the postcards. But how? The only explanation she could think of was that one of the other girls had shown it to a friend. But hey, she'd wanted to meet new people, so the more the merrier, right? She laughed out loud at the craziness of the situation – from zero friends to *three* replies to her postcards. But now it was over to her again. She needed to respond, and she needed to get it right. She opened the note app on her phone and started composing a rough draft of a message.

Hey! Thanks heaps for responding to my postcard. My name's
Jazz and I'm fourteen years old and I've just moved to the UK
from Australia. I came up with the idea for the postcard after a
truly terrible first week at my new school. Basically, my parents
have sent me to this super-posh private school where everyone
talks like the Queen and no one wants to be friends with me and
I feel like everyone's judging me because I don't come from the
UK and…

She paused. Who in their right mind would turn up after an introduction like that? She sounded way too pathetic and needy. She deleted the draft and took a deep breath. Maybe it would be better if she replied to each of the messages individually. She had another look at the email from P – the girl with the dog – clicked on reply and started to type...

Dear P,

Thanks so much for responding to my postcard, and no, the questions weren't a trick. If you would like to solve the rest of the mystery, I'll be holding the first Moonlight Dreamers meeting at the end of the public beach by the lagoon tomorrow (Sunday) at 4 p.m. Hope you can make it...

Jazz

She reread her response. It was definitely better to keep it short and sweet and maintain the mystery. She took a deep breath and pressed SEND. Then she replied to Hope.

Dear Hope,

Thank you so much for responding to the postcard. I was so sorry to hear about your health condition – that sucks. I totally get what you say about not all of us being in the gutter. Some people definitely have a swankier gutter than others, that's for sure. The Moonlight Dreamers is all about celebrating people who don't fit in so I really

hope you'll be able to come to our first meeting tomorrow (Sunday)
at 4 p.m. at the end of the public beach by the lagoon. I'd really
like to meet you.

Jazz

And now for the surprise bonus email. She reread it and quickly typed a reply before her nerves got the better of her.

Hey! Thanks so much for responding to my postcard. I totally get
what you're saying about the school gutter! This is definitely not a
prank or a marketing gimmick; I just wanted to meet some fellow
free spirits. I badly need things to change too! I'd love it if you could
come to the first meeting of the Moonlight Dreamers on the end
of the beach by the lagoon at 4 p.m. tomorrow (Sunday). Hope to
see you there…

Jazz

Jazz sat back on her bed and looked out of the window. The emails were sent. It was too late to back out now. She looked up into the night sky and there in the darkness she saw the faintest glimmer of a star.

Chapter Ten

Portia walked purposefully along the seafront with Reggie tugging hard on his lead. She couldn't let him off yet, though, just in case she needed to make a swift exit. She'd already walked him up to the i360; now she was making her way back to Shirley's road. To any passer-by, she was merely a dog walker out on a stroll. Her plan was to case the end of the beach for any sign of the mysterious postcard sender as she walked by. If she saw anyone who looked like an axe murderer she would simply carry on walking. If the mystery sender turned out to be someone from her school, she would only join them if they met three key criteria. One, they had to be in her year or above. Two, they had to look interesting. Three, they had to be a girl. After lengthy research, admittedly based mainly on her brothers, she'd come to the depressing conclusion that boys were an intensely annoying species.

As she drew level with the final section of the public beach, she saw a woman wrestling with a screaming toddler and her heart sank. Had she accidentally been invited to join some kind of club for stressed-out mums? But then she saw a flash of colour against the brown and grey of the pebbles. A girl with short blonde hair wearing a bright blue tracksuit was sitting at the very end of the beach, leaning against the fence that partitioned off the private beaches on Shirley's road. Portia didn't recognize the girl from school, although she did look vaguely familiar. Time for Part Two of her cunning plan.

She headed down the steps and let Reggie off his lead. She could still use the cover of being a dog walker and she would wait and see if the girl made any move to greet her. As the harassed woman dragged her toddler past Portia, Reggie raced right by where the girl was sitting, over to the water's edge. Portia casually strolled over, eyes fixed on the sea. She felt like she was in one of those old-school spy comics, about to meet a contact to pass on a secret coded message. When Portia drew level with the girl, she shot her a quick glance. The girl was looking down into her lap. Hmm, maybe she didn't have anything to do with the postcard after all.

Portia scanned the beach. Apart from the woman and toddler, there was no one else in sight. She checked the time on her phone. It was four o'clock exactly. What if she'd been the victim of some kind of elaborate prank? She looked up at the seafront to see if anyone was filming her on their phone but there was no one there. She looked back at the girl and this time she met her gaze.

Portia felt a jolt of recognition. It was the girl who lived next door to Shirley – the "problem child". Could she be the mystery postcard sender? But how had she got the card into her bag? Then Portia remembered seeing her the other day when she'd been scooping Reggie's poop. Could the girl have somehow slipped the card into Portia's bag while she wasn't looking? The plot thickened!

Hope sat at the counter of Donuts and Discs nervously stirring a straw around her glass. It was almost four o'clock. Almost time for the mysterious meeting on the beach. When she'd received a reply to her email, she'd felt excited. The person who sent it – "Jazz" – seemed genuine, and she got what Hope was trying to say about not everyone being in the gutter. But now that it was getting close to the time that they were supposed to meet she wasn't so sure. She glanced at the clock on the wall behind the counter. It was now or never. Her mum, Petra, came out from the kitchen.

"Hadn't you better get going?" she asked with a smile.

Hope had told her she was going to meet a school friend. Petra had seemed so relieved at this news she'd practically thrown a party. Again, Hope felt a wave of doubt.

"I'm not sure I'm going to go," she said quietly.

"What?" Petra's face fell. "But why?"

Hope shrugged. "Can't be bothered."

"Oh, Hope, I hate seeing you like this."

"Like what?" Hope felt her hackles rise.

"So down. I know you're missing Meg but you need to carry on with your life."

Why? Hope wanted to ask. *What's the point in carrying on with half a life?*

"Or is it the HCM?" Petra placed her hand on Hope's arm. "Are you worried still? I totally understand if you are and, like I keep saying, you can always talk to me about it."

"How are my favourite girls? Or two of them anyway."

Hope turned to see Pete coming into the café, holding a large cardboard box. He'd been to a record fair and by the looks of it had stocked up on a lot of new vinyl to play in the café. He plonked the box down on a table and came over and hugged Hope.

"I got some gems today." He went behind the counter and planted a kiss on Petra's lips. "Hello, gorgeous."

Hope sighed. She knew she was lucky to have parents who were still as in love as hers were but now Meg had gone she felt like a third wheel. Before their family of four had worked so well – Petra and Pete, Hope and Meg. Now it was Petra and Pete, with their annoyingly cute matching names, and Hope, the spare part. She got off her stool.

"See you in a bit."

"So, you *are* going?" Petra looked at her hopefully.

"Yeah. I won't be long, though."

Pete looked at Petra questioningly.

"She's meeting a friend on the beach," Petra said, giving him a knowing look. Parent code, no doubt, for, *Hallelujah, she's finally getting a life*.

"That's great, love. Have fun!" Pete beamed at her. Clearly

they both couldn't wait for her to get out from under their feet. The broken daughter.

"I have to go to the toilet first," she muttered, feeling dangerously close to tears.

Portia watched, poker-faced, as the girl scrambled to her feet and smiled, looking slightly embarrassed. "Hey, I'm Jazz."

"You're the mystery postcard sender?"

"Yep." She laughed and her face flushed. "But I promise you I'm not crazy. I just..." She broke off and looked at Reggie, who, as per usual, was yelping at some seagulls. "I just wanted to make some new friends and I wasn't sure how else to do it."

Portia could think of many ways to make new friends but none quite as ingenious and daring as this. It instantly made her warm to her. "Did you put the card in my bag when I was cleaning up after Reggie?"

"Yes. I hope you don't mind." Jazz stuffed her hands in her tracksuit pockets. "I didn't know how else to approach you. I figured that this way you'd only come and meet me if you wanted to. Thanks so much, by the way."

"Are you kidding? It was way too intriguing not to."

"For real?" Jazz smiled at her hopefully.

"Yeah. When I first got here, I had a horrible feeling I'd been invited to a local branch meeting of Stressed-Out Mums Anonymous." She gestured at the woman further along the beach. Her child was now stripping off his clothes and trying to run into the sea, screaming at the top of his voice.

Jazz laughed. "That does not look like fun."

"So, what's the idea then?" Portia asked as they both sat down on the pebbles. "Who are the Moonlight Dreamers?"

"It was something my cousin started a few years ago, when she wanted to meet people. I moved to the UK recently, and she suggested I did it too. I wasn't sure at first but then I started school and..."

"Say no more! What school are you at?"

"Cedars College. You don't go there, do you?" she asked hopefully.

Portia shook her head. "No, I'm at Brighton Secondary, it's a state school. So, did you give anyone else a card?"

"Yes. I'm not sure if she'll show up, though." Jazz glanced across the beach. "And, uh, there might be someone else coming too."

Portia followed her gaze to a tall girl with tanned skin and long dark hair, picking her way across the pebbles towards them. She was wearing a black fedora hat and denim shorts and a vest top beneath a long open trench coat. The girl looked over and gave them a slightly awkward smile.

"Are you – did one of you write the postcard?" she called above the shriek of a seagull. Reggie turned to look at her then continued chasing after the gull.

Jazz stood up, almost losing her footing on the pebbles. "Yes. Hi, I'm Jazz."

"Hey, I'm Allegra."

Portia stayed seated and studied the girl. Normally, she took an instant dislike to girls as beautiful as Allegra. It wasn't because she was jealous – Portia had way more interesting things in life to think about. It was more that she'd always found super-attractive people to be quite boring. She had a theory that because the whole world revolved around idolizing good-looking people they never had to bother developing personalities. But Allegra's outfit definitely indicated that a personality could be lurking. It was so original, especially the bright purple trainers with the words FREE SPIRIT stamped on the sides in silver. She gave her a welcoming grin. "I'm Portia. I got one of the mysterious postcards too."

"Can I – can I ask how you got yours?" Jazz asked Allegra.

"I found it – on a table outside Donuts and Discs." Her smile faded. "Was I meant to find it, or was it meant for someone else?"

"Well, I…" But before Jazz could finish there was the crunch of feet on pebbles and Portia saw a pale girl with vivid auburn hair making her way towards them.

"Hope?" Jazz said.

Allegra quickly turned to look and said something under her breath. Portia couldn't be sure but it sounded very like, "Oh no."

Portia grinned. It would appear that things were about to get *very* interesting.

Chapter Eleven

Hope wasn't sure she'd ever experienced such a wide range of emotions within a couple of seconds. First, fear as she approached the girls, then excitement and recognition as she realized one of them was the Australian girl she'd served in the café, curiosity as she'd checked out a girl in black with short dark hair, olive skin and an elfin face, and, finally, horror. The girl standing with her back to Hope was Allegra.

"Oh," was all she could say, as her face let her down again and started to burn.

"I'm Jazz," the Australian girl was saying. "I'm the one who left the postcard at the café."

But Hope couldn't process that now. All she could think was that her nemesis was standing right there in front of her, clearly a part of this Moonlight Dreamers thing. A terrible thought occurred to her. Was this some kind of prank? Revenge for not giving Allegra's friends free doughnuts? She glanced behind her for any sign of Alf and the other boys. Thankfully, apart from a woman and her screaming child, their part of the beach was empty.

But now Allegra was speaking. "Did you leave the card at the café for her?" she asked Jazz. Was it Hope's imagination or was Allegra's face burning too?

"Yes, but I'm really happy you found it," Jazz replied.

Hope tried to compute what must have happened. She'd been in such a rush to get away from Allegra and her friends that she'd left the card on the table. Allegra must have picked it up when she hurried inside. Hope pictured Allegra and her friends all reading the card and laughing. But what was Allegra doing here? Another terrible thought occurred to her. What if she was here to spy on Hope? No doubt tomorrow she'd report back to her friends in school about the secret meeting Hope had attended on the beach for people who were proud to be different. And the good feeling she'd had when she'd read the postcard would sour into something bad.

"I need to go," she muttered, turning to leave.

"Wait, please." Jazz grabbed her arm. "Can I at least explain what this is all about?"

"That would be good," Allegra said.

Anger surged through Hope. She turned and glared at Allegra. "Why? So you can tell everyone in school tomorrow and make fun of me?"

"What? No!" Allegra looked genuinely shocked.

"Do you guys know each other?" Jazz asked.

"Yep." Somehow Hope managed to refrain from adding, *Unfortunately.*

"I'm really sorry about what happened yesterday," Allegra said, looking Hope straight in the eye. "I came back to the café yesterday evening to apologize but you weren't there. That's when I found the card."

"Apologize for what?" the girl with short brown hair asked.

"There was a bit of a misunderstanding," Allegra replied.

"A misunderstanding?" Hope echoed incredulously.

"I'm sorry Alf was a total idiot." To Hope's surprise, Allegra looked truly remorseful. Her anger subsided slightly.

"Who's Alf?" the brown-haired girl asked. A dog came running over and jumped up at her legs. The girl took a treat from her pocket and popped it into the dog's mouth.

"He's – he's my boyfriend," Allegra replied glumly.

So, Alf and Allegra were an item. That made sense, Hope thought. Allegra was the Queen of Cool and Alf was the king. If only she hadn't left the postcard on the table, this wouldn't be happening. It would just be her and the other two girls, both of whom seemed OK. But she definitely didn't want to be a part of any club that had Allegra as a member.

Strewth, Jazz thought to herself as she watched the tension crackle between Hope and Allegra. In all of the worst-case scenarios she'd imagined for this meeting, the chances of two deadly enemies turning up had never occurred to her. But hadn't Amber experienced something similar? Hadn't her friends Sky and Rose hated each other at first? Jazz had to do something to make the peace, to get them both to stay. At least Allegra seemed to be trying to make amends for whatever this Alf guy had done.

"He shouldn't have talked to you like that," she was saying to Hope now. "I'm really sorry."

Jazz looked at Hope anxiously, willing her to accept the apology.

"OK," Hope said, with a slight nod of her head.

There was an awkward pause.

"Well..." Jazz glanced around the group. "Shall we sit down? Just for a minute. So I can tell you what this is all about and then, if you don't like the sound of it, there's no pressure to stay."

"Fine by me." Portia sat back down and the dog leapt into her lap.

"OK," Allegra said, looking at Hope.

"All right," Hope murmured.

Jazz breathed a sigh of relief. Now she just had the small challenge of trying to sell them the idea of hanging out together.

"So, I just recently moved here from Australia," she began.

"Cool!" Allegra smiled appreciatively.

"And the truth is, I've been finding it a little hard to fit in. I'd been hoping I'd make some friends at school, but so far, no good."

"She goes to Cedars," Portia interjected, as if this explained everything.

"Ah, OK," Allegra said and Hope nodded knowingly.

"Is there something I should know?" Jazz half joked.

"Some of the kids who go there suffer from rich-kid syndrome," Portia explained. "They think that just because their parents can afford thousands a term in fees that it makes them better than everyone else."

"I hate playing them at netball," Allegra said. "They're so arrogant."

To Jazz's relief, Hope nodded. Much as she didn't like hearing her parents had sent her to some kind of school for spoiled brats, it was good to see Allegra and Hope bonding over something – even if it was because her school sucked.

"Well, you can rest assured I'm not in the least bit stuck-up."

"Of course you're not, you're Australian," Portia said. Jazz wasn't quite sure what she meant by this but she liked the fact that there was a warmth in the way she said it.

"So you gave out the postcards because you wanted to make friends?" Allegra asked.

"Yeah, but not just any old friends." Jazz smiled at her. "I wanted to meet kindred spirits. The kind of people who would respond to some random postcard they found on a café table."

"Or smuggled into their backpack." Portia laughed.

"Yes, exactly."

"Why did you call it the Moonlight Dreamers?" Allegra took off her hat and twisted her long dark hair into a thick braid.

"It was something my cousin started a few years ago. It helped her meet her best friends and achieve her dreams. She suggested I try it too." Jazz held her breath. This was the bit she'd been most worried about. Would the other girls think she was crazy? But to her relief Portia and Allegra were both nodding.

"That sounds cool," Portia said.

"How did it help her achieve her dreams?" Allegra asked, looking really interested.

"She and her friends used to share what their dreams were at their meetings and then they'd help each other plan how to achieve them. I was thinking…" Jazz broke off for a moment. "I was thinking maybe – if you like the sound of it – we could do that too… I mean, we could each share a dream we have now, as a way of getting to know one another." She hardly dared look at the other girls as she waited for their response.

"I have so many!" Allegra said with a sigh.

"Really? Like what?"

"Well, to travel the world for a start." Allegra picked up a pebble and turned it over in the palm of her hand.

"Where would you go?" Jazz asked.

"Everywhere! But Paris, New York and Peru to begin with. And I'd love to go to Australia," she added with a smile.

"Awesome." Jazz felt a warm glow inside. "If you need a tour guide, I'd be happy to show you the sights."

Allegra laughed. "How about you? What are your dreams?"

Jazz resisted the urge to say that she dreamed of going home. She didn't want them to know that she hated their country. "Right now, it's to surf." She looked out at the ocean and sighed. "But it doesn't seem like there's much surfing to be had here."

"They hire out paddleboards in the lagoon," Hope said.

Again, Jazz had to fight the urge to appear ungrateful. "Yeah, I saw that. Maybe I'll try it. How about you?" She smiled at Hope. "Is there anything you dream of doing?"

Hope looked down into her lap. "Not really."

"There must be something," Portia said.

Hope shook her head.

She looked upset, so Jazz decided not to press it. "How about you, Portia?"

"I'd like to save all the animals who are being cruelly treated," she replied, hugging Reggie to her. "I appreciate that's quite an unrealistic dream but if I can at least help some of them it will be worth it. I'd love to work in a dog rescue centre but you have to be sixteen to work there so I donate money to one every month instead."

"Cool." Jazz grinned. "Is he a rescue dog?" She gestured at Reggie.

"No. Shirley, his owner, got him from a breeder. She's one of my dog-walking clients – the only one now, thanks to my parents."

"What do you mean?" Allegra asked.

"I set up a dog-walking service at the start of the summer holiday, when my parents told me I wasn't allowed to get a pet dog."

So Portia didn't live next door after all, Jazz thought.

"That's really cool that you set up your own business," Allegra said.

"Thank you." Portia grinned.

Jazz was so pleased to see the two girls bond. Hope was the only one who looked like she really didn't want to be there, and Jazz's spirits fell as she watched her shifting uncomfortably on the stones.

Chapter Twelve

Allegra tucked her coat under her legs like a cushion in an attempt to get more comfortable. At first she really hadn't been sure about this Moonlight Dreamers thing, especially when Hope had rocked up with a face like thunder, but now she'd heard Jazz and Portia talk about their dreams, she was won over. She and her best friend Chantelle never had conversations like this. All they talked about was who they liked, who they hated and what they were doing at the weekend. But with these girls – or Jazz and Portia at least – the lens on the world seemed a whole lot wider. And she really liked the notion of having a secret group of friends with whom she could be her true self and talk about her true feelings. Then a horrible thought occurred to Allegra. What if Hope told people at school about this? What if Chantelle and the others found out about it?

"So, when my cousin and her friends started the Moonlight Dreamers, they came up with some rules," Jazz said, taking a velvet bag from her backpack and pulling out a piece of paper. "I thought I could read them to you. We don't have to follow them or anything but it could be a good place to start."

"Cool!" Portia said and Allegra nodded. Hope was still staring into her lap.

"The Moonlight Dreamers is a secret society," Jazz began. "Members must never speak a word of its existence or what happens at the meetings to others."

Allegra was relieved. Maybe that would stop Hope from blabbing.

"Meetings will begin with members reciting the moonlight quote from Oscar Wilde."

"What's that?" Portia asked.

"It's the quote my cousin used on her postcard to get members. I used the starlight quote instead, so maybe we could use that."

Allegra smiled. "I love that quote."

"Rule three: this quote is the Moonlight Dreamers' motto and must be memorized by members and never forgotten.

"Rule four: all members must vow to support the other Moonlight Dreamers in the pursuit of their dreams — always."

Allegra nodded – she liked this one.

"Rule five: Moonlight Dreamers are proud of being different. Being the same as everyone else is a crime against originality – the human equivalent of magnolia paint."

"Magnolia is the worst colour ever!" Portia exclaimed. "So dull."

Allegra chuckled. "You'd like my bedroom then. I painted it turquoise!"

"Were your parents OK with that?" Portia stared at her wide-eyed. "I've been begging my mum and dad to let me paint my bedroom but they keep saying no. I think they're worried I'll paint a mural of my favourite graphic novel heroes." She laughed.

"Yeah. My mum pretty much lets me do my own thing." In spite of Portia's and Jazz's looks of appreciation, Allegra couldn't help feeling slightly flat about this.

"Awesome," Jazz said, before continuing. "Rule six: Moonlight Dreamers tell one another everything – even the bad stuff. Especially the bad stuff."

Allegra pondered this. It would be good to have some-where she could confide her darkest fears and regrets, somewhere she wasn't always worried about looking and being perfect. If it was just her and Jazz and Portia, she could see herself being comfortable enough to open up but the thought of telling Hope anything private made her cringe. Clearly Hope was feeling the same from the way she was shifting about awkwardly.

"And finally, rule seven," Jazz said, "Moonlight Dreamers never, ever give up."

"Never give up what?" Portia asked.

Jazz shrugged. "Pursuing their dreams, I guess. We don't have to stick to these rules; we can always make up our own – that's if you want to?" She looked around at them hopefully.

"I like it," Portia said.

"Me too," said Allegra. She glanced at Hope.

"Sounds good," Hope said quietly but she hardly sounded enthused.

Allegra wondered if maybe Hope wouldn't come again and relief flooded through her, quickly followed by guilt. Hope was probably only being so miserable because Allegra was there, and Jazz had meant the postcard for her. She sighed. This was one of the best things to have happened to her in ages. It was as if a light had come on at the end of the dark and boring tunnel that was her life. The *moon*light at the end of the tunnel, she thought to herself with a grin.

"So, what do you say, we meet up again properly this coming week?" Jazz asked.

"Great!" Portia agreed enthusiastically.

"I'm in," said Allegra.

They all looked at Hope. "Sure," she said, still not making eye contact.

"That's great!" Jazz looked so happy and Allegra instantly warmed to her. Plus this was the first time she'd got to know someone from Australia and she couldn't wait to find out more. "How about Thursday evening?" Jazz suggested. "We could go to my place if you like. I only live down there, at number twelve." She nodded in the direction of the private road at the end of the beach.

Wow, so Jazz lived on "Millionaire's Row" as it was known locally. It made sense, if her parents had the kind of money to send her to Cedars. Allegra's interest grew. She'd always wondered what the houses down there were like.

"Well, that's nice and easy for me." Portia grinned. "I can come round after walking Reggie. His owner lives next door to Jazz," she explained to Allegra and Hope. "Jazz slipped the postcard in my bag while I was scooping his poop."

"No way!" Allegra laughed.

Jazz grimaced. "I was so scared you were going to see me. I thought you'd accuse me of trying to steal your purse or something!" She clapped her hands together and grinned. "OK, then, let's meet again on Thursday."

As the girls stood up Hope's mind twisted into knots. *Say something! Do something!* her inner voice pleaded. *Show them that you aren't totally miserable.* But once again, her awkwardness had struck her dumb. *They'll be better off without you anyway*, she told herself as they started walking over the pebbles back to the seafront. *For a start, you're the only one who hasn't got a dream.* And she still wasn't comfortable hanging out with Allegra, in spite of her apology. When they got to the promenade, Portia clipped a lead on Reggie and Hope had the horrible realization that Portia and Jazz would be going in the opposite direction – leaving her alone with Allegra.

"Which way are you guys going?" Jazz asked.

"That way," Allegra mumbled, gesturing along the front towards Hove, clearly as delighted as Hope by the fact that they were about to be left together.

"Cool. See you Thursday then."

The girls shared a slightly awkward goodbye and then it was just Hope and Allegra. At first they walked in total silence. Then Allegra cleared her throat.

"I really am sorry about what happened yesterday."

"Don't worry about it," Hope muttered, looking at the floor. However sorry Allegra might be, the fact was that Alf was her boyfriend – she chose to go out with him.

After what was only a couple of minutes, but felt like ages, they reached the steps in between the beach huts leading to the lagoon.

"See you tomorrow at school then," Allegra said as Hope turned to go.

"Yeah, see you." Hope ran down the steps, hot with embarrassment and anger. It was so unfair. The postcard had been meant for her and yet somehow it had found its way to Allegra, who was now crowding her out of something that could have actually been good. Jazz seemed really nice and Portia too.

When she got to the café, the closed sign was hanging in the door. She let herself in to discover her parents slow-dancing to a love song on the record player. Great. Everywhere Hope went she felt out of place. And the one person who'd made her feel like she was a part of something was miles away at university, no doubt slotting in effortlessly in the way Meg always did.

"Hello, love," Petra called, breaking away from Pete. "Did you have a nice time?"

"Yeah," she replied shortly. "Can we go home now, please? I'm really tired."

"Of course." Petra came over and put her arm round her. "Are you OK?"

"Yes." But the truth was, Hope had never felt further from OK.

Chapter Thirteen

As Portia cut down the back alley leading to her street, she felt happier than she had in ages. She felt more alive than she had in ages. Finally, in the hamster wheel that was her life, something different had happened, *someone* different had happened – or three someones to be precise. Jazz was her favourite. How could she not admire someone with so much nerve, setting up a secret society and stuffing a postcard about it in her bag right under her nose? Allegra seemed pretty cool too – for a beautiful person. She definitely had some personality at least. Hope was the only one she wasn't sure about but only because she'd barely said a word. She wondered what the beef was between Allegra and Hope. It seemed pretty serious. One good thing about her brothers was that they didn't have the patience to bear grudges. If you did something to annoy them, they wanted to sort it out there and then – usually in the form of a wrestling match.

Just as Portia was going past one of the tall gates in the alleyway, she heard a yelp, like an animal in pain, which stopped her in her tracks.

"You stupid bloody dog," she heard a man say, followed by another yelp.

Portia peered through the narrow gap between the gate and the wall and into the back garden. All she could see was a thin strip of stubbly grass. Then there was a flash of white fur as a dog ran past, whimpering. Had it been hurt? She waited, dead still, hardly daring to breathe. She heard the man mutter something, then a door slammed. She shifted slightly, trying to get a better view. The dog was standing on the patio by the back door, shivering and whimpering. Portia stood there for a moment, trying to figure out what to do. What she wanted to do was break down the gate or clamber over the wall and scoop that poor dog up and bring it home with her. She would bathe it and feed it and shower it with love and rename it Scamp – she'd always wanted a dog called Scamp – and they would live together happily ever after.

Her daydream came screeching to a halt as she remembered how her parents always got in the way of her dog-related happily-ever-afters. She also knew that right now she was feeling angry and nothing good ever seemed to come from the things she did when she was "hot-headed", as her mum called it. The last time Portia had been accused of being hot-headed – when one of the twins had put some home-made slime inside her lunchbox and she'd retaliated by drawing floral tattoos all over his WWE action figures (she honestly hadn't known it was a permanent marker) – her mum had taken her metronome from on top of the piano and plonked it down in front of her. "I know the twins can be challenging but instead of losing your cool, I want you to put this on and breathe in time with the beats. It's what I do," she added with a grin, before setting the metronome at its slowest tempo.

"But he put slime in my lunchbox," Portia wailed.

"Breathe in time," her mum repeated, looking at the metronome.

Portia had watched the metronome slowly going back and forth but instead of breathing, she'd said, *Life's so unfair*, over and over in her mind in time with the beat.

But now, in the alleyway, she pictured the metronome in her head and slowed her breathing. There was no point trying to get into the garden. Knowing her luck, she'd be arrested for breaking and entering. Perhaps she could keep an eye on the house though, check it over the next few days for any other signs of animal cruelty. And if she found any she could report the owner to the RSPCA.

Portia marched off down the alleyway, counting the houses as she went. When she got to the end, she followed the road round to the front and started counting again. The house with the dog had been the seventh one along. When she got there, she instantly felt sad. Unlike the other houses on the street, with their shiny front doors and pristine gardens, this house was faded and shabby. The white paintwork on the wall was chipped and peeling, and yellowing net curtains hung in the windows. Even the droopy weeds poking up through the cracks in the garden path seemed to be hanging their heads in sorrow. The thought of a dog having to live in a house like this with an owner that yelled at it, and possibly worse, filled Portia with dread. She quickly got out her phone, jotted down the name of the street and the house number painted on the wheelie bin by the door, and set off for home.

Allegra smelled him before she saw him – the second she stepped into the hallway the overpowering scent of cheap aftershave flooded her nostrils. Her heart didn't just sink, it plummeted right down to the soles of her feet. From along the hallway, in the living room, she heard the tinkle of Magdalena's laugh, her fake laugh, the one she always used on men she liked, which was pretty much all of them. Allegra was about to slip into her bedroom when the living room door opened and a man walked into the hall. He had pale ginger hair and even paler blue eyes and he was wearing low-slung jeans, a thick gold chain and snowy white trainers. His NWA T-shirt strained over a paunch. Allegra grimaced.

"Oh, hello," he said, with a grin. "So who are you, then?" He eyed her up and down, his gaze lingering for a little too long on her legs.

"Her daughter," Allegra snapped, marching into her bedroom and slamming the door behind her. Magdalena had *promised*. After what happened a couple of months ago, when she'd brought home that creepy man from a club, who'd barged in on Allegra in the bathroom. She'd promised: no more men in the house unless Allegra was away. Allegra couldn't believe she'd gone back on her word – and so quickly. Her eyes smarted as all of the positivity she'd been feeling since the Moonlight Dreamers meeting began to fade. She'd turned her phone off while she'd been on the beach; now she turned it on again to find three new messages from Alf.

Hey, guess who scored the winner today at football! :-)

I don't care, she thought angrily. *How about asking me how my day's been?* Not that she'd ever tell Alf about the Moonlight Dreamers. There was no way he'd get it. He'd probably just laugh. She read his next message and her mood softened.

I no ur out with ur friends but let me no if u want to meet up later. My old man is pissing me off

Allegra had never met Alf's dad but she'd gathered they didn't get on well. One time last year Alf had come into school with a black eye, which he claimed he'd got playing football, but the rumour that had buzzed around the canteen and school corridors was that he'd got it from his dad. She opened his third message, which he'd sent ten minutes ago.

Had to come out to clear my head. Down at beach in our shelter. Meet me? Xx

Her heart felt like a bud opening. Alf never put kisses on his texts. And the fact that he'd written "our" shelter hinted that maybe he did have a romantic streak after all. Perhaps she'd been too swift to judge him. Yesterday he'd been showing off in front of his friends but maybe if it was just the two of them things would be different. Better.

She heard the pop of a cork followed by a shriek of laughter from her mum. The thought of having to spend Sunday evening listening to her and Mr Midlife Crisis getting it on made Allegra's stomach turn. She replied to the text.

On my way. xx

She found Alf sitting huddled inside the shelter, the hood on his tracksuit top pulled up against the driving wind coming in off the sea. He appeared so happy to see her she felt her heart unfurl some more.

"You OK?" she asked, sitting down beside him.

"Not really. My old man's been on a bender. He does my head in when he gets that drunk."

"That's crap. If it's any consolation, my mum's been doing my head in too."

"Why, what's up?" He looked genuinely concerned.

"Oh, she just went back on her word about something."

"Some people should never have been allowed to become parents," Alf muttered, looking at the waves jumping and frothing at the sea wall. "Like, he yells at me that I ruined his life, but I didn't choose to be born. You ruined your own life, mate." He picked up a pebble and flung it out into the water.

"Did he really say that to you?"

"He's always saying that to me. I can't wait till I'm old enough to leave."

"Me too!" Allegra exclaimed. Finally, she was feeling the spark of a connection with him that she'd craved.

"So, who were you with today?" he said.

"Just some friends from another school."

"Oh yeah?" He took hold of her hand. His fingers were icy cold. "How do you know them?"

Damn! She'd been dying for him to be more interested in her life, why did he finally have to show an interest in the one thing she wanted to keep to herself?

"From a dance class I used to go to," she said quickly. There was still no way she was going to tell him the truth. She just had to pray Hope kept her mouth shut in school.

"Oh, right." He looked away. "Do you wanna go somewhere?"

"Where?"

"I dunno, somewhere more private." He grinned. "We could go to the lagoon. There'll be no one down there now it's getting dark."

Her heart sank. It was obvious what he had on his mind. But she didn't want to make out; she wanted to carry on talking to him, bonding over their unfit parents.

"Could we go and get something to eat instead? I'm starving."

"Sure. Chips?"

"OK."

"We could take them to the lagoon."

As they stood and started walking along the front, disappointment returned to Allegra, like a chill fog rolling in from the sea.

Chapter Fourteen

Today is the day I turn everything around, Jazz declared to herself as she marched into school. *Today I will make friends with at least one of these stuck-up Poms if it kills me!* Buoyed up by the success of the first Moonlight Dreamers meeting, she felt a new spring in her step. She'd been so worried the meeting would be a disaster but it had turned out so much better than she'd expected; maybe the same could be true when it came to school. She just had to believe, that was all.

Jazz visualized herself gliding into her form room and rows of smiling faces turning like sunflowers to greet her. *Today, everyone will like me*, she said to herself as she walked in the door. But no one even noticed. Even Beth, who'd been forced to be her buddy on day one, was engrossed in conversation with another girl, both of them hunched together over a textbook. Jazz felt her newfound positivity start to wane. *You can do it*, she told herself. *You talked to complete strangers yesterday, didn't you? And they didn't hate you.* She sat down and glanced at the two girls next to her. They both looked so polished and well put together.

"I can't wait to ride Prince Caspian again," one of the girls was saying. The other girl caught Jazz's gaze so she jumped at the opportunity.

"Hey, did you guys have a good weekend?"

They completely ignored her and continued talking. But surely the girl had seen her; she'd been looking straight at her. Maybe she hadn't realized Jazz was talking to her, although, really, there was no one else she could have been talking to. She waited until the girl glanced over again and this time made sure she was speaking loudly. "Did you have a good weekend?" *Hmm, maybe a little too loud*, she thought, as her words bellowed out.

"Pardon?" The girl looked at her like she was insane.

"Did you have a good weekend?"

"Oh – yes." The girls looked away and carried on talking. This was the final straw.

"Wow!" she said sarcastically.

"Wow, what?" The girl looked back at her, her expression as cool as ice.

"I guess it's true what they say about you Brits: you're so arrogant you still think you own half the world. Well – newsflash – you don't!"

Unfortunately, the whole class fell silent just as Jazz was delivering her volley, and her words rang loudly around the room. She turned to see Mr Montague standing in the doorway.

"What on earth's going on?" he asked, his bushy grey eyebrows knotting together in a frown.

"Sorry," she muttered, staring at her desk. *Good one, Jazz. Way to make friends – make the whole class think you hate them and their country.*

"Dare I ask what prompted that outburst?" Mr Montague said, sitting down at his desk.

"Nothing," Jazz said, painfully aware that this made her look even more stupid, but she didn't want to add "snitch" to the list of reasons for her classmates to hate her.

"Jessica? Becky?" He looked at the other girls.

"Don't ask me," Prince Caspian Lover replied. "She just, like, flipped out."

"Hmm." Mr Montague sighed. "Can you come and see me at first break please, Jasmine?"

Jazz nodded glumly, burning from a mixture of indignation and shame.

Hope swallowed her beta blocker with three gulps of water. Then she tapped her hand on her leg three times. She'd started this ritual a couple of weeks after being diagnosed. Three had always been her favourite number – she wasn't sure why – but since she'd had to start taking meds, it had taken on a greater significance, becoming a lucky charm, somehow easing her fear. If she just did things three times, the beta blockers would prevent all the terrible outcomes she'd found on Google – after being told not to google her condition by her consultant. Today, at the thought of having to go to school and face Allegra and Alf, she felt in need of extra protection. So she checked her keys were in her bag three times and tapped on the front door three times before leaving.

Outside, the sun was shining brightly and the sky was the vivid shade of blue unique to September. It instantly lifted her spirits – until she got to the bus stop at the end of her road and saw Allegra leaning against an advert for a designer watch. A THING OF BEAUTY… it read. How apt. Allegra was so beautiful she could even make their horrible burgundy school uniform look good, especially the way she'd accessorized it with a pair of DM boots and a vintage leather biker jacket. But it didn't matter how nice she looked, she still filled Hope with dread. But it was too late now, Allegra had seen her, and she was waving.

"Hi," Hope said glumly as she reached the bus stop.

"Hey. I was hoping to catch you here."

"You were?"

"Yeah." Allegra smiled. "I was just – uh – wondering…"

They both fell silent. Hope watched the cars passing by, wishing she could magically transport herself away from this awkwardness.

"You're not…" Allegra broke off again. It was weird seeing the Queen of Cool looking so awkward. "You're not going to say anything to anyone are you – about yesterday?"

Ah, so that's what she was worried about. She didn't want any of her stupid friends to know she'd been hanging out with Hope.

"I mean, I know it's supposed to be secret anyway but I just wanted to check. I won't be telling anyone."

I bet you won't, Hope thought crossly. Allegra had seemed really enthusiastic at the meeting but she was so fake.

"Don't worry, I won't say a word," Hope said. "And I won't be going to another meeting, so you can relax."

"Why not?" Allegra looked shocked.

"It's not my kind of thing." It pained her to say this because, actually, if Allegra hadn't showed up, the Moonlight Dreamers meeting would have been very much her kind of thing.

"You're not just saying that because I was there, are you?"

"Don't flatter yourself," Hope snapped. "Not everything revolves around you, you know."

"What's that supposed to mean?"

Hope could feel the blood pulsing in her ears. *Don't get angry, stay calm*, she urged herself, thinking of her heart having to work extra hard to pump the blood. "Nothing. It doesn't matter." She glanced at Allegra. Up this close she could see dark shadows beneath her eyes that her concealer hadn't quite been able to hide.

"Look, I know you've got cancer," Allegra snapped back, "but that's no excuse to act like this."

Allegra's words stung like a slap. *For your information, I don't have cancer, I have a heart condition — a heart condition that is the most common cause of sudden cardiac death in people under thirty!* she wanted to yell. But what was the point?

Allegra was totally self-absorbed. How could Hope ever expect her to understand?

Thankfully, at that moment their bus appeared. Hope felt in her pocket for her pass, tapping it three times with her fingertips to try and calm herself. She stood back and let Allegra get on first and when she headed upstairs, Hope stayed on the lower deck, counting the seats until she got to the third row. She sat down and peered out of the window. The beautiful sunshine casting everything in a golden glow suddenly seemed like a cruel trick.

As soon as school was over, Portia rushed home and got changed, then set off to go and walk Reggie. When she got to the alleyway, she counted the back gates until she reached the seventh house. She peered through the crack between the gate and the wall. There was no sign of the dog on the patchy grass. She looked up at the house. The back was just as shabby as the front, the white walls yellowing with age. What if the dog was just as neglected too? What if the owner forgot to feed them? Or take them for a walk? It broke her heart to think of it. As she carried on walking, her phone pinged. She took it from her pocket to see an email from Jazz, titled, **MOONLIGHT DREAMERS MEETING TWO**.

G'day, fellow Dreamers,

I sincerely hope your Monday hasn't been as lousy as mine!
I just thought I'd get in touch because while I was spending my

lunchbreak in the disabled toilet – trying to avoid everyone I've managed to piss off in one morning (my entire class AND teacher – don't ask!), I discovered that this Thursday when we're meeting is going to be a full moon, and apparently the full moon is the perfect time for making dreams come true. I promise you I'm not a wack job, I just really, really want my life to get better and I have a hunch that you do too. So get your thinking caps on and let's come up with some dreams. We have a firepit on our beach at home, so maybe we could toast some marshmallows as well as manifest our dreams. ☺ I'm so looking forward to seeing you all again!

Jazz xx

Allegra could always tell what kind of mood her mum was in by the colour of her nail polish. Red meant she was in the mood for romance. When she wore pink, she was feeling girly. And when she wore funky colours, like the bright baby blue gleaming from her nails right now, she was trying to be cool and, as she liked to put it, "down with the kids".

"Coffee or tea, honey?" Magdalena called, as she danced the kettle over to the sink. The hair salon was closed on Mondays so Magdalena was always extra cheery.

"Can I have a hot chocolate, please?"

"Of course!"

Allegra sighed. Magdalena was only being super nice to her because she knew she'd messed up, bringing that guy back home.

"Marshmallows?" Magdalena asked and Allegra nodded. The dipping sun shone in through the window, causing the gold highlights in Magdalena's hair to glow. There was no denying she was beautiful, but she was also forty-one years old. Just like Alf thought that some people shouldn't be allowed to become parents, Allegra felt strongly that those who did have kids should act their age and stop acting like teenagers.

"So, I hear you met Jonny." Magdalena sprinkled some tiny pink and white marshmallows into the hot chocolate froth.

"Yep."

"He's really nice, Allegra, not like…"

"All the others?" Allegra filled the pause.

"There haven't been that many!"

"Hmm."

Magdalena placed the hot chocolate in front of her and sat down. "My life isn't over, you know. I am entitled to have some fun."

Yes, but not at my expense, Allegra internally yelled. She took a sip and instantly the tension in her shoulders eased a little. It had been a crappy day right from the start when she met Hope at the bus stop. Allegra had set off for school fully intending to try and make things better between them. But Hope had made it clear within seconds that making things better was definitely not on her to-do list. Allegra grimaced as she recalled their prickly conversation. She shouldn't have snapped at Hope. She couldn't begin to imagine what it must be like to have cancer, especially if the latest rumour sweeping the school was correct and Hope had a rare brain tumour.

"I think you'd get on really well with Jonny," Magdalena continued. "He plays in a band."

"Oh yeah." Allegra raised her eyebrows. "Anyone I've heard of?"

"No, they're more of a tribute act. They play at weddings and parties."

"Wow," Allegra replied sarcastically.

Instantly, Magdalena's smile faded and she looked hurt. "So, how was school?"

"Boring, as usual."

"Never mind, you'll be out of there soon, darling."

Allegra wasn't sure if it was the fact that her period was due, or that things had gone so badly with Hope, or that she was still dating a boy who made her soul sag with disappointment, but for some reason, her mum's response sent a bolt of anger through her. Even though she couldn't wait to be out of school, part of her wished she had a mum who encouraged her in her education. Wasn't that what parents were supposed to do? She took her phone from her bag and saw that she had a new email from Jazz. It was the email equivalent of a hot chocolate, filling her with warmth.

"I was thinking," Magdalena continued. "Maybe you could come with me to one of Jonny's gigs."

Allegra looked up from her phone. "What, at some randoms' wedding?"

"No! They play in local pubs too."

"Er, hello, I'm only fourteen."

Magdalena smiled. "I'm sure we could get you in if you were with the band."

"They're a wedding tribute band, Mum, not BTS."

"Who?"

"Exactly."

Again, Magdalena looked wounded.

Allegra stood up. "I'm going to go do my homework."

"OK. I'll start making the dinner."

"What, *you're* going to cook?" *Stop being such a bitch!* Allegra's inner voice cried. But she couldn't help it, she was so angry at everything she couldn't contain it.

"Yes, actually, I am!" Magdalena replied defiantly.

"Great." Allegra picked up her hot chocolate and bag and trudged down the hallway to her bedroom. She flung herself on her bed and read the email from Jazz and her entire body exhaled. The thought of going to Jazz's house and sitting on her beach and toasting marshmallows and talking about their dreams instantly soothed her. It was as if Jazz knew exactly what she needed to hear.

Allegra went over to the window and looked out at the estate below. She'd been feeling bad about finding the postcard intended for Hope, but what if she'd been meant to find it too? What if it was destiny that made Hope leave it on the table, so that Allegra could discover it? She thought back to one of the summers she'd spent with her abuela Sofia in Spain when she was younger. One morning they'd gone up to a village in the mountains and sat outside a café drinking tiny glasses of Spanish hot chocolate, which was so thick and velvety it was like someone had melted a chocolate bar and poured it into the cup. Fortified by the sugar rush, Allegra had confided in her abuela that she wished she knew her dad. Sofia had placed one of her tanned, wrinkled hands on hers and smiled.

"Don't worry, not knowing him must be part of God's plan for you," she'd said in a hushed voice. "He has a plan for all of us."

"I thought God wanted mums and dads to be married and stay together for ever," Allegra had responded.

"Hmm, that's what the Church wants for us."

"But isn't it the same thing?"

Sofia smiled enigmatically. "God has a plan," she said again. "And that plan includes the obstacles we meet, because they're what make us wiser and stronger."

As Allegra recalled her abuela's words now, she felt an ache inside as strong as hunger. Why had she demanded to stay home this summer, instead of going to Spain, as usual? She knew of course that the answer to that question had been Alf, and her burning fear that if she was away for the summer holiday she would miss her chance and some other girl would snare him. How had she got it so wrong? She looked back at Jazz's email. She didn't really believe in

God but what if the universe did have some kind of plan for everyone? And what if finding Jazz's postcard had been part of that plan? She clicked reply and started typing.

This sounds great! Thank you. And sorry you've had a rubbish day. If it's any consolation mine's been pretty crappy too, but I can't wait till Thursday. I'm in need of some serious dreaming too!

Allegra xx

Hope sat down at her favourite table in Donuts and Discs, tucked away in the corner by the shelves of records, and took out her books. She knew that it was a tragic state of affairs when you actually looked forward to doing your homework, but in English they'd started *Lord of the Flies* and she was perversely enjoying the darkness of the novel. Just as she was about to start reading, her phone began to ring. She felt a surge of joy as she saw from the caller ID that it was Megan. They hadn't spoken since last Thursday, which was the longest they'd ever gone without talking.

"Hey, Megs," she said, answering the phone.

"Hey, Hopeless."

"Ha ha!" She pretended to be annoyed but really it was wonderful to hear her sister's voice calling her by her nickname. "How's uni life?"

"It's amazing. Freshers' week has just started so it's crazy busy. I've joined about seven hundred societies."

"I've told you fifty billion times not to exaggerate."

Megan giggled. "Seriously, though, there are so many fun things to join. On Wednesday night I'm going to a hula-hooping class and I've joined the Pun Society."

"The Pun Society?"

"Yep."

"What, so you all sit around making puns all night?"

"I guess so. I'll find out next Tuesday when it begins. Don't worry, I'll report back. How's everything with you? What's it like being back at school?"

"Not great, to be honest." Hope glanced out of the window. The sunshine had brought crowds of people to the lagoon, sitting on the banks of grass eating ice creams. "It all feels so different now – you know, now I've been diagnosed."

"What did you say?"

Hope heard a peal of laughter ring out in the background at Meg's end, followed by loud cheering.

"Hey, guys, I'll just be a minute," Meg called in a sing-song, YouTuber-style voice Hope had never heard her use before. "Sorry, sis," she said quietly, in her normal voice. "I'm going to have to go, my flatmates are back and we're going for a curry. I'll call you another time for a proper chat. When things are quieter. If things ever get quieter! Love you!"

"Of course. Have fun at the curry. Hope it isn't dahl. Dahl, dull, get it?" Hope giggled. "Feel free to use that at the Pun Society."

But Megan had already gone and Hope's joke fell into

the silence like a stone. She was about to put her phone away when she saw that she had an email from Jazz. It was about their second meeting, on Thursday – the meeting Hope had vowed to Allegra she wouldn't be attending. She thought of the other three girls meeting on the beach to toast marshmallows and talk about their dreams. Then she thought about Megan, laughing and joking with her brand-new friends in her brand-new voice. And then the camera in her mind panned back to her, alone and watching from the sidelines. She tapped her leg three times beneath the table. *It's going to be OK. You're going to be OK. Tap, tap, tap ... one, two, three.*

"Here's your smoothie, love." Petra arrived at the table, and put down a glass of something so green it looked radioactive. Hope couldn't even have one of her beloved milkshakes any more because she was supposed to be keeping her defective heart healthy.

Somehow she managed to squeeze out the words, "Thanks, Mum."

As soon as Petra left, Hope clicked on Jazz's email and then REPLY.

Hi, I'm really sorry but I'm not going to be able to come to any more meetings. I don't really think it's my kind of thing. I hope it goes well.

Hope

She knew it was the right thing to do, the *only* thing to do, given the circumstances, but she really felt like crying. She opened her copy of *Lord of the Flies* and began to read, wanting to lose herself in a far worse world of savage bullying and the struggle to survive. But no matter how many times her eyes scanned the page, the only thing she could hear was her own voice telling her how stupid she'd been.

Chapter Fifteen

There are times in life, Jazz thought to herself, *when it really feels as if you are the butt of the world's worst joke.* She stared at her dad. Then she stared at what he was holding.

"What do you reckon?" he said, beaming widely, like he'd just presented her with a cheque for a million dollars.

"A paddleboard?" she said, incredulously. *An effing paddleboard!* the voice in her mind echoed.

"Yeah, seems like they're all the rage round here." He grinned and looked out of the kitchen window at someone slowly paddling in the distance.

And you think that's a good thing?

"And I know how much you love being out on the water."

Yes, surfing! she wanted to yell. *Not wading in slow motion.* But he looked so pleased with himself she didn't have the heart to tell him what she really felt.

"Thanks, Dad."

"You're welcome, darlin'." He leaned the board against the wall, next to the paddle. "Right, I'd better get back to the studio."

"Sure."

Jazz poured herself a glass of orange juice and went out onto the deck. The sunshine had transformed the ocean from its usual murky grey to a bright jade green and it was so calm the waves looked like the faintest of wrinkles. If only there was some groundswell, some real waves she could ride. She sat down and looked at her phone. She'd had another reply to her email, this time from Hope. Her spirits lifted and she clicked Hope's message open.

"Oh man!" she sighed as she began to read. Was the Moonlight Dreamers really not her kind of thing? Or was Hope's backing out more to do with her clash with Allegra? If that was it, it was really annoying. She wondered if Hope was at her parents' café. She downed her juice and hurried back inside.

Down in the lagoon a handful of people were having paddleboarding lessons on the lake. *Don't bother*, Jazz wanted to warn them. *Not unless you want to die of boredom.* Paddleboard? More like paddle-*bored*! She chuckled at her ingenious play on words. There was no sign of Hope at the tables outside the café, so Jazz went inside. One of the songs from her parents' favourite movie, *Grease*, was playing and a couple of guys in wetsuits were sitting at the counter, munching on doughnuts. The setting sun was pouring through the windows in shafts of red and gold. It was a scene that felt so familiar that for a moment, Jazz could have been back at home. She looked around. If it hadn't been for the bright auburn hair, she might not have noticed Hope tucked away at the table in the corner, her nose in a book. Jazz went over and cleared her throat. Hope looked up. Jazz was encouraged by her grin, although it quickly faded to a frown.

"I just replied to your email," she said.

"I know. That's why I'm here."

"Oh."

"Do you mind if I sit down?" Jazz gestured at the chair opposite.

"Not at all."

Jazz sat. "Can I ask you something?"

"Sure." Hope put her book down.

"Did you really mean what you said about the Moonlight Dreamers not being your thing?"

Hope's face flushed.

"I don't mean to pressure you or anything it's just that, well, as my dad would say –" she deepened her voice – "I know a pile of possum dung when I smell it."

Hope stared at her blankly.

"I wasn't sure that was the real reason," Jazz quickly explained. "I mean, if you genuinely don't think it would be fun, then of course you don't have to come. But I just had a feeling it might be more to do with the issues you've got going on with Allegra." Jazz took a breath. She really hoped she hadn't upset her. To her relief, Hope nodded.

"It is a little awkward between us."

"Dang it." Jazz sighed. "I left the postcard for you."

"Really?" Hope's emerald eyes widened. With her red

hair and high cheekbones, she was really striking. When she wasn't scowling.

"Yeah. You looked really interesting – I wanted to get to know you better."

"Seriously?" The tips of Hope's cheeks flushed pink and although Jazz couldn't be certain, what looked suspiciously like a smile was twitching at the corners of her mouth.

"Yeah. Are you sure you don't want to come? Maybe it would help you guys patch things up."

A frown returned to Hope's face. "I don't know."

Just then a woman with red hair came over to the table, beaming at Jazz like she was a long-lost friend.

"Hey," she said, before turning to Hope. "Is this a friend from school, sweetheart?"

"No," Hope replied.

"I am a friend, though – a new friend," Jazz said, smiling. She'd get Hope to be friends with her if it killed her.

"Ah, that's lovely. I'm Hope's mum, Petra. Can I get you anything? Doughnut? Drink? My treat," she added.

"Really?"

"Of course. Any friend of Hope's is welcome here."

"Thanks." Jazz ordered a lemon cheesecake doughnut and a chocolate milkshake. "I don't know how you aren't the size of a house owning this place," she joked once Hope's mum had gone back over to the counter. "I'd be having doughnuts for breakfast, lunch and dinner."

Hope sighed and looked at the green dregs in the bottom

of her glass. "Yeah, well, I'm not supposed to eat too many of them any more."

"Shit, I'm sorry. Is it to do with your heart condition?"

"Yeah."

"That sucks."

Hope gave her a weak smile. "Yeah, it does."

"And it's even more reason why you should join us on Thursday."

Hope still looked unconvinced. It was time for Jazz to pull out her trump card. She really hoped it would work. She took the book of Oscar Wilde quotes out of her bag. "OK, so we're gonna play a little game called What Would Oscar Say?"

"What's that?"

"It's a game my cousin taught me, when she was telling me about the Moonlight Dreamers. It's kind of how the whole thing came to be."

"OK." Hope looked interested. This was good.

"Basically, you have to think of a problem you're facing and turn it into a question. Then you turn to a random page in the book for your answer. When I first played it, I was feeling really homesick, so my question was: how will I ever feel happy again?"

Hope still looked interested. Jazz breathed a sigh of relief and passed her the book. "You don't need to tell me what your question is. Just get it really clear in your mind."

"OK." Hope stared at the book for a moment, a look of concentration on her face. "All right, I've asked it."

"Great. Now turn to a random page." Jazz watched as Hope flicked the book open. *Please, please let it work.* "The quote you've turned to is the answer to your question." She held her breath. *Come on, Oscar. Don't let me down!*

At first Hope's face remained expressionless but then, to Jazz's surprise, her eyes filled with tears. Oh crap. Had she made things even worse?

"How – how did you do that?" Hope stammered. A tear escaped and rolled down her cheek.

"What do you mean?"

"How did it open on exactly the right page?"

"I'm not sure how it works; it just does. It's like the book knows exactly what you need to read. Can I – can I see what you got?"

"Sure." Hope passed the book across the table and Jazz read the quote.

Live! Live the wonderful life that is in you! Let nothing be lost upon you. Be always searching for new sensations. Be afraid of nothing.

"Wow! That's a good one," Jazz murmured.

"OK," Hope said quietly. "I'll come to the meeting."

Chapter Sixteen

Allegra's last class of the day on Thursdays was English, which was perfect as she was in a higher set than Chantelle and her other friends and could slip out of school without them noticing. But, just as she reached the school gate, she heard a piercing whistle, followed by Alf calling her name. *No!* At lunchtime all the talk had been about meeting up in the park that evening. Chantelle had nicked some cigarettes from her mum and Alf had apparently acquired a bottle of vodka. Even if she didn't have a Moonlight Dreamers meeting to go to, Allegra would have wanted to give the meet-up a steer: a bunch of school kids drinking and smoking in a park seemed kind of tragic. If and when she ever drank and smoked, she wanted it to be somewhere exotic and exciting and adult – like a nightclub in New York, or one of those super-atmospheric bistros in Paris.

"Yo, Leggy!" She bristled at the sound of Alf's voice, right behind her. "Where are you off to in such a hurry?"

She took a deep breath and turned to look at him. He smiled at her. His school jumper was tied around his waist and his shirt was undone at the collar, his tie loosened. At the sight of his dimples, she felt that old fluttering in the pit of her stomach. She had to ignore it, though. She needed to listen to her head, and it was telling her to come up with an excuse quick.

"I — I have a dental appointment," she said as a girl with a mouthful of braces walked by.

Alf's smile faded. "How come you never said?"

"I'm saying now." Her reply came out shorter than she'd intended but she didn't like the way he asked. Why should she tell him her every move?

"Do you want me to come with you?"

"What, to the dentist?"

"Yeah." He shrugged. "I dunno, I thought you might need some moral support. Last time I went I needed three fillings. Mind you, I hadn't been for, like, five years."

No doubt sending his son to the dentist was way down Alf's dad's list of priorities. Magdalena might be intensely annoying at times but she always made sure Allegra kept her dental and doctor's appointments.

"It's OK," she replied, putting her hand on Alf's arm. "Thanks, though."

"No worries. I'll see you down the park later, yeah?"

Allegra saw Chantelle and the other girls heading their way. Crap, it would be way harder lying to them.

"Yeah, probably. Unless I'm in too much pain from the dentist." Perfect. This would be her excuse.

"All right. Text me, yeah."

"Yeah. Gotta go." She turned and practically ran down the street, ignoring Chantelle's shrill voice calling out after her. It was the strangest feeling, literally running away from the people she called her friends. She hoped her intuition was right and tonight's meeting on the beach would help her feel better...

After yet another day in school being blanked by all and sundry, Jazz could not get out of the building fast enough when the final buzzer rang. Since her outburst, word seemed to have spread throughout her year that she should be avoided like the plague. *Suits me fine*, she felt like calling over her shoulder at her fellow students as she raced through the school gate. *I have other friends now. Or, at least, I hope I will...* she thought nervously.

When Jazz got home, she found her mum in the kitchen drinking a cup of tea.

"Hello, sweetheart," Cheryl said with a smile. "How was your day?"

"OK."

"Are you still having your new friends over tonight?"

"Yeah." Jazz joined her at the table. "Can I ask your advice about something?"

"Of course."

"What would you do if you had two friends who didn't really like each other, but you really wanted them to get on well so that you could all hang out together?"

"Oh." Cheryl looked thoughtful for a moment. "Well, when your Aunt Jess and Aunt Dani fell out and didn't speak for about a month, your grandad locked them in a room together." She chuckled. "He said, they'll either kill each other or make up, but either way we won't have to put up with their feuding any more."

Jazz laughed. "Sounds like Grandad. What happened? I mean, obviously they didn't kill each other but did they make up?"

Cheryl nodded. "Yup. It took a while but when they finally emerged, they were best mates again and it was as if all the fighting had never happened."

Jazz thought of Allegra and Hope. She had the strongest hunch that if she put them in a room together, they'd both storm out in seconds.

"Why do you ask? Have a couple of your friends fallen out?"

"Yeah, a couple of the girls who are coming round tonight. I'm worried it'll be a little tense."

"What'll be a little tense?" asked Mikey, breezing into the room.

"A couple of the girls Jazz is having over tonight have had a bit of a falling-out," Cheryl replied.

"Oh dear. I could always tell them a few jokes."

"No!" Jazz and Cheryl cried in unison.

"Wow!" Mikey feigned a hurt expression. "How about I cook you all something on the barbie then? No one can stay mad long when my grilling's on the menu."

"Geez, someone's got tickets on themselves," Cheryl chuckled.

"What? It's true!" Mikey exclaimed. "It's why you married me, isn't it? You couldn't resist my honey-glazed spare ribs."

"Well, it certainly wasn't for your humility." Cheryl went over and planted a kiss on his cheek.

Jazz cleared her throat. "Can I – uh – ask you both a huge favour?"

"Uh-oh." Mikey looked at Cheryl and raised his eyebrows. "Don't say yes till we know what it is."

"What is it, sweetheart?" Cheryl asked.

"Well, you know how you uprooted me and brought me thousands of kilometres away from my friends?"

"Yes," Mikey replied, looking wary.

"And I agreed and hardly complained at all."

"Er, that's because you refused to speak to us for about a month," Mikey retorted.

"Shh!" Cheryl nudged him in the ribs. "Go on."

"And now I've been pro-active and made some new friends. Or, at least, I think I have."

Her parents nodded.

"I just need you guys to do me a favour and not ruin things."

"How would we ruin it?" Mikey exclaimed in mock indignation.

"I mean it, Dad. I need some privacy. So when they get here, can you guys stay in the living room or your bedroom?

I'm going to take them out on the beach, so please promise me not to come out on the decking."

"OK then." Mikey looked at Cheryl. "Are we really that embarrassing?"

"'Fraid so, darling," she laughed.

As Portia made her way along the alleyway, she stopped outside the seventh gate and peered through the crack. At first she thought the garden was empty again but then she saw a streak of white fur.

"Hello," she whispered. She heard the rustle of paws on grass and panting. "I hope you're OK."

A shiny black nose sniffed at the gap, and the dog started to whimper. Was it trying to tell her that it was being mistreated? That it needed to be rescued? She remembered the doggy treats she had in her backpack for Reggie and threw one of them over the gate. A moment later she heard an enthusiastic chomping. Had her suspicions been correct? Did the dog's owner forget to feed it? What if it was starving? Portia's heart ached at the thought. Then she had a brainwave.

"Don't worry, I'll be back again tomorrow," she whispered, throwing over a couple more treats.

Hope stared at her reflection in the bathroom mirror at Donuts and Discs. "You can do this," she told herself. "You *have* to do this!"

She'd wanted to speak to Allegra after their English class, to tell her that she would be coming to the meeting after all, but Allegra rushed out before Hope had even finished putting her books in her bag. Maybe she had somewhere else to go, Hope thought. Maybe she wouldn't be going to the Moonlight Dreamers meeting after all. That would definitely be the best possible outcome. She thought of Allegra not turning up at the meeting and tapped the top of her head three times. Seeing herself do this in the mirror made her blush. Was she going crazy with all this tapping? It had made sense when it was about taking her meds but now it seemed to be spiralling out of control. The trouble was, it was the only thing that seemed to keep her ever-pressing fear at bay. She gave her hair three strokes with her brush then turned to go.

Outside, the sun was setting and a huge moon was glowing orange in the sky. Hope remembered what Jazz had said about the full moon helping to make dreams come true. Surely that couldn't be right. The moon didn't have that kind of magical power. But then it did control the sea's tides, she thought as she watched the sea lapping against the shore, so clearly it was powerful. Jazz had sent another email telling them to meet her at the end of the seafront – at the entrance to the private road where she lived ("Millionaires' Row" as Hope's dad called it). It was funny, Jazz didn't seem like a rich kid at all, even though she must be, living there and going to the elite Cedars College. Maybe it was the fact that she was Australian – they always seemed so down to earth. As the private road came into view, Hope's pulse quickened, instantly triggering fearful thoughts about her heart. To take her mind off it she started counting her steps. *One, two, three... One, two, three...* And slowly but surely her heart rate returned to normal. *I have just as much right to be here as Allegra*, she told herself, *if not more, seeing as Jazz had meant the postcard for me.*

Reading that quote in Jazz's book had had a profound effect on her. When Jazz had asked her to think of a question, *How am I supposed to live with HCM?* had instantly formed in her mind. The quote she'd turned to, with its command to *"Live!"* was so insistent that she couldn't possibly ignore it, and she took it as a sign that she should definitely come to the meeting.

"Hope!" she heard someone call from behind her. She turned to see Portia hurrying along the seafront. She was wearing a black baker boy cap, which – along with her elfin face and button nose – gave her the air of a street urchin from a Dickens novel.

"Hey," Hope replied with a smile, relieved it wasn't Allegra.

"How are you doing?" Portia asked as she drew level.

"Good, thanks."

"It's great to see you. I wasn't sure..." Portia broke off.

"What?"

"Nothing. It's great to see you," she repeated with a grin.

They continued walking and Hope felt a pang of anxiety as she noticed Allegra leaning against the PRIVATE sign at the beginning of Jazz's road. As always, she looked effortlessly beautiful, in a long floral dress, denim jacket and a silver pair of Converse.

"Hope!" she said, looking surprised as they approached her.

"Hi," Hope replied.

"It – it's really good to see you."

Hope scanned her face for any sign that she was lying but Allegra looked more shocked than anything. Before any of them could say anything else Jazz came jogging up the road towards them.

"Hey," she called. "Am I glad to see all of you!"

Chapter Seventeen

Jazz led the girls through the kitchen and out onto the deck. Below them, on the beach, the firepit was blazing, casting dancing shadows on the pebbles. Thankfully her parents had kept their word and were upstairs in their bedroom.

"Wow, this place is amazing!" Allegra exclaimed, looking around. "You're so lucky to have your own beach."

"I know," Jazz replied. "Come on, let's go down there."

She led the girls onto the beach and they made their way over to the firepit. "Hopefully this can become our regular meeting place," she said, looking at the others shyly. "I'd love to share it with you."

"I gladly accept that invitation!" Portia exclaimed.

"Me too," Allegra agreed.

"And me," Hope said quietly.

Jazz felt a tingle of relief. She so badly wanted them to like her. After the disaster at school they were the only thing stopping her from drowning in despair. She glanced at Hope, staring out across the water at the moon.

"The moon looks epic tonight, doesn't it?" Jazz said, following her gaze.

"Why's it so orange?" Allegra asked.

"Apparently it's something to do with the atmosphere at this time of year," Jazz replied. "I googled it earlier."

"Cool." Allegra smiled.

Jazz picked up a flask. "Anyone want some hot chocolate?" The girls nodded and she poured it out. "I have marshmallows for toasting too."

"Awesome!" Portia exclaimed.

Jazz handed out the toasting sticks. "So, how's everyone's week been?"

"Crap," Allegra said instantly.

"Really?" Jazz looked at her, surprised. Allegra looked so perfect and graceful she imagined her gliding through life like a swan, everything around her effortlessly falling into place.

"What happened?" Portia asked.

"Oh, my mum's been a pain and —" she glanced sideways at Hope — "I just have a few personal issues to deal with. How about you?" Allegra asked Jazz, seeming eager to change the subject. "It sounded from your email like you've had a pretty grim week."

"Don't!" Jazz exclaimed. "I somehow managed to piss off the mean girls in my class and make it look as if I hate all Brits. I don't hate all Brits," she quickly added, passing around the bag of marshmallows. "Only the stuck-up ones."

"Yeah, well, you'll probably find a lot of them at Cedars." Portia grinned.

"Tell me about it. How's your week been?"

"OK." Portia's smile faded. "I think I might have discovered a dog that's being abused, though."

"What?" Jazz exclaimed. The other girls looked at Portia, clearly shocked.

"On my way home from meeting you guys on Sunday I heard someone yelling at a dog in their back garden. I couldn't see if the dog was being physically abused but it was whimpering a lot, so I'm keeping the garden under surveillance. If there is anything dodgy going on, I'm going to hand their arses to the RSPCA."

Jazz bit her lip to stop herself giggling. Portia might be tiny but she was clearly a bit of a spitfire. She turned to Hope. "How about you, Hope. How's your week been?"

Before Hope could say a word, Allegra's phone beeped. She looked at it and frowned. Hope was now also frowning – at Allegra.

"I've definitely had better weeks," she said.

"How come – if you feel like sharing?" Jazz asked tentatively. It was so hard to get Hope to say anything and she didn't want to blow it.

"I'm really missing my sister," Hope said quietly. "She's gone off to—"

Allegra's phone beeped again. And again.

"Sorry!" she exclaimed.

"Maybe we should all put our phones on silent," Jazz suggested.

"I already did," Hope replied, again glaring at Allegra.

"I'll turn it off." Allegra put her phone back in her pocket. "Sorry."

"So, you were saying, Hope," Jazz said. "Your sister's gone off to…"

"To university. In Manchester."

"Where's Manchester?" Jazz asked.

"Miles away, up north," Hope replied. "So she might as well be on the other side of the world. She's my best friend," she added, staring into the flames.

"Aw, that sucks." Jazz gave her a sympathetic smile. "I know all about missing best friends. And mine really are on the other side of the world."

"I'm sorry," Hope said. "That must be so hard."

"Yeah, well, that's what this is all about, isn't it?" Jazz smiled at the girls. "To make new friends and make our lives better."

"I'll drink to that," Portia said, raising her mug of hot chocolate.

"Me too." Allegra clinked her cup against Portia's. And then all the girls were cheers-ing, even Hope. Jazz breathed a sigh of relief. So far, so good.

Allegra took a sip of hot chocolate and tried to swallow down her anger. She knew it was partially her fault for not putting her phone on silent before the meeting but did Alf really have to message her three times in a row? Normally, he kept his messages to a minimum, but tonight for some reason he seemed desperate for contact, asking her where she was and when she'd get to the park – even though she'd messaged to tell him she wouldn't be coming. It was as if he knew she was somewhere else, and didn't really have toothache.

She looked at the other girls. Hope didn't fit into her friendship group and there was no way Portia would either. She studied Portia's old-style cap, polo neck, jeans and boots as if through Chantelle's eyes. She imagined Chantelle shaking her head and saying, "What a freak."

Allegra shifted her gaze to Jazz, who was asking if they'd given any more thought to their dreams since they'd last met. Of all the girls, Jazz was the one Allegra could most imagine fitting into her group at school, mainly because she was so sporty-looking, and being athletic instantly won you points in the popularity league table. But Jazz had been the one to set up the Moonlight Dreamers – something none of her friends would ever do. She sighed. Maybe she belonged in the park with the others. Maybe she should never have come. She tuned back in to the conversation.

"I thought it might be cool if we turned it into some kind of challenge," Jazz was saying. *Turned* what *into some kind of challenge*? Allegra hadn't been paying attention. "Like we all set ourselves a weekly goal, to help us make our dreams come true."

"What if…" Hope began, before breaking off and glancing at Allegra. "What if your dream is impossible to achieve?" she murmured.

"What do you mean?" Portia asked, pushing a marshmallow onto her stick and holding it over the fire.

"Well, the only dream I can think of right now is not…" she broke off.

Allegra froze. Was she about to say that her only dream was not being somewhere with Allegra?

"Not what?" Jazz asked gently.

"Not having a heart condition," Hope practically whispered, staring into the flames. "But I'll never be able to change that."

Allegra felt her pulse quicken. So Hope didn't have a brain tumour or cancer. But a heart condition sounded just as serious.

"A heart condition?" Portia's brown eyes widened.

"Yeah. I was diagnosed with it at the start of the summer and, let's just say, I wish I hadn't been."

"That must have been such a shock," said Portia.

"Yes and no," Hope replied. "I have something called HCM, which basically means that part of the wall of my heart has become too thick and stiff and it makes it harder to pump blood around my body. It's a hereditary condition. My mum has it so there was always a chance me or my sister might get it. We've had to go for yearly tests ever since we were ten. That's how I found out I'd drawn the short straw." She gave a dry laugh.

Allegra felt awful. When Hope's illness had been a school rumour it hadn't seemed real, but now she could see the pain and fear on Hope's face, it was all too real, and all too horrible. "I'm really sorry," she said, quietly.

Hope looked at her questioningly, like she wasn't sure Allegra was being authentic. Finally she gave a small smile. "Thank you."

"So, what does it mean?" Portia asked. "Like, have you had to change anything about how you live your life? Sorry if that's a dumb question," she added.

"It's not dumb," Hope replied. "I'm not allowed to take part in competitive sports any more. I can do some exercise but not anything that puts too much strain on my heart."

"Is that why..." Allegra paused. "Is that why Ms Sykes made you goalkeeper in PE?"

"Yes. She thought it would be OK as it's a lot less running, but it still freaked me out." Hope put her toasting stick down in her lap and sighed.

Allegra thought back to how annoyed she'd been when Ms Sykes put Hope in her position. She was ashamed at what a brat she'd been. "I'm really sorry," she said again.

"What exercise are you allowed to do?" Jazz asked.

"I can go for a jog, or cycle or swim. I just..." Hope broke off and stared into the flames.

"Who wants to do competitive sport anyway?" Portia said before popping her toasted marshmallow into her mouth. "I think sport is highly overrated," she added with a grin.

To Allegra's relief, Hope giggled. Then her smile faded. "I

just feel as if everyone else is getting on with their lives and I'm being left behind."

"Are there other things you can't do?" Allegra asked.

Hope looked at her blankly.

"Apart from sport, I mean."

"Well, no, I can still go to school – unfortunately."

Allegra wasn't sure if this last word was directed at her personally but she decided to ignore it. "And you're still allowed to go out and do things with friends?"

"Yes…"

"So you can still have dreams then." Allegra smiled, but to her dismay Hope was now glaring.

"Yes, I can dream I don't drop dead from heart failure!"

"OK," Jazz said quickly. "Who needs some more marshmallows?"

Allegra put a marshmallow on her stick, her face smarting. Thankfully the sun had now set so hopefully the others wouldn't see her embarrassment. She really didn't understand Hope. Surely it was obvious she was trying to be helpful. Maybe Hope preferred feeling sorry for herself, which was hugely ironic, given her name. Well, if she wasn't interested in anything Allegra had to say there was no point in trying.

"So, Allegra," Jazz said, "do you have any dreams you'd like to share?"

Allegra took a deep breath. Part of her wanted to get up and march out, all the way to the park, where her real friends were. But something kept her rooted to the beach. Maybe it was the moon, pushing on her like it pushed and pulled the tides. She looked up and drank in its orange glow. She'd wanted to share her feelings about Alf, and how she dreamed of being free of him. But now that things had gone wrong with Hope again there was no way she was going to open up about something so personal, and something Hope could use against her in school. She searched her mind for a softer, safer dream.

"I'd love to go and visit my abuela – my grandma – in Spain," she replied.

"I'd love to go to Spain too," Portia said. "To protest against the bullfights. They're so barbaric and inhumane, I can't believe they're still allowed to go on."

Allegra felt something inside her closing down. She shouldn't be here; she wasn't welcome. Hope clearly hated her guts and now Portia was slagging off Spain. Even though Allegra had been born in Britain she felt Spanish through and through.

"I'd love to go to Spain too." Jazz grinned. "Barcelona looks amazing."

"It is!" Allegra felt a prickle of hope. "And so is Andalusia, where my family are from. My grandma has an olive grove that's almost a thousand years old and she lives in a town surrounded by mountains." She looked out dreamily across the water. Just talking about Spain instantly made her feel better.

"It sounds great." Portia handed her the bag of marshmallows, as if extending an olive branch.

Allegra smiled. "It is."

"Awesome dream," Jazz said. "Maybe you could take us all with you too."

Allegra smiled but the thought of taking the hopeless Hope to Spain made her cringe. There was no way that was *ever* going to happen.

Chapter Eighteen

Portia held her marshmallow over the fire and silently cursed herself. Why had she said that thing about bullfighting? Yes, it was a barbaric sport but she'd sounded as if she was criticizing all of Spain and all Spanish people. *There's a reason why you prefer hanging out with animals and characters from novels*, she reminded herself. *It's way harder to upset them.* And Allegra *had* been upset, she was sure of it. She'd seen the way her face had fallen. And coming so soon after Hope had bitten her head off, it couldn't have been worse timing.

"So, how about you, Portia?" Jazz asked. "Got a dream you'd like to share?"

Portia wasn't sure about Jazz turning this whole dreams thing into a challenge, like it was some kind of sport. She wasn't sure she could summon a dream to order. But this was still way more interesting than anything she'd done recently so she decided to play along.

"I guess my biggest dream right now would be to have a dog of my own but… Well, my parents have made it clear that they'd be more likely to allow me to open a crack den, so I guess that's the end of that."

She was relieved to hear Allegra giggle.

"Yeah, parents can be annoying like that," Jazz said, glancing up at the house.

"What if you just brought a dog home with you one day?" Allegra suggested. "Told them you'd found a stray? Maybe if they saw it they wouldn't be able to say no."

"Yeah." Jazz grinned. "Especially if it was a super-cute puppy."

"You don't know my parents," Portia replied. "Everyone thinks they're lovely and kind – and they are, most of the time – but when it comes to pets, they have hearts of stone. They'd just put it in the car and take it to the nearest rescue centre."

"You need to develop a life-threatening health condition," Hope said. "Then they'd let you have anything you want to try and make you feel better."

"Oh – uh – well, that might be a bit extreme," Portia replied.

"I was just joking." Hope looked away, clearly embarrassed, and began tapping her hand on her leg.

Portia quickly laughed. She glanced across at Shirley's house next door and thought of Reggie. If only he were here now, slathering her with kisses. He'd never take offence at anything she said.

"Is there anything else you'd like?" Jazz asked.

"Not really," Portia replied, deciding that it was probably safest to stop talking. "How about you?" she asked.

"Hmm, well, like most of you, I have a dream that I can't see coming true."

"What is it?" Hope asked.

"To go surfing again." Jazz gazed out at the sea, glimmering in the amber moonlight. "I miss it so much I'm starting to get serious withdrawal. Last night I dreamed that I'd married a surfboard called Bruce!"

Allegra laughed. "To be fair, a surfboard wouldn't be too bad a husband. At least you'd never have an argument and they'd never want to know what you were doing or where you'd been. And if they were annoying you, you could just stick them in a cupboard."

"I wish I could do that with my brothers," Portia muttered.

Jazz laughed. "Good point! Anyway, I've decided that since I can't go surfing right now, I'm going to have a go at paddleboarding."

"Fun!" Allegra exclaimed.

"Are you sure?" Jazz stared at her. "It looks so boring."

"My brother Darius saw a seal once when he went paddleboarding," Portia said.

"No way?" Jazz's eyes lit up. "What, here in Brighton?"

"Yeah. He said it swam alongside him."

Jazz grinned. "That's so cool."

"I don't think it happens very often, but you never know," Portia said, relieved to have said something that made someone happy rather than annoyed for once.

"Thank you. You've just made paddleboarding a whole

lot more appealing." Jazz reached into her bag and brought out some paper and pens. "OK, so I have it on very good authority that if we want our dreams to come true, we need to write them down and then let them go."

"What do you mean, let them go?" Portia asked.

"Well, we could burn them…" Jazz gestured at the fire. "Or we could tear them up and throw them into the water."

"Let's burn them," Portia said quickly. It sounded way more dramatic.

"Yes," Allegra agreed and Hope nodded.

"OK." Jazz handed each of them a piece of paper and a pen.

Portia stared out at the sea thoughtfully. Then she wrote, *Rescue the dog I heard in the alleyway from its cruel owner.* She glanced around at the others, who all had their heads bent, writing away – even Hope, she was glad to see.

"Let's fold them up," Jazz said.

"Do you think we ought to say something?" Allegra asked. "You know, to make it feel more official?"

"Sure," Jazz agreed. "What do you reckon?"

"How about we ask the moon for help?" Allegra suggested.

"Great idea," Portia said with a grin, looking up. The moon was so huge and orange it felt like a scene from a sci-fi graphic novel, with the moon being a mysterious fiery planet.

The girls fell silent for a moment, then Jazz giggled. "I'm not exactly sure what to say!"

"How about, *Dear Moon, please use your mystical powers to*

help us make our dreams come true," Portia suggested.

"Sounds good to me," Jazz agreed.

Allegra and Hope nodded.

Yes! Portia thought to herself. Maybe she was capable of this whole human interaction thing after all.

"Should we say it all together?" Jazz asked.

"I think so," Portia replied. "I reckon that'll help increase the moon's powers."

The four girls stared into the flames.

"On three?" Jazz suggested.

"Yes," Hope agreed. Portia was relieved to hear her speak.

"One … two … three…" Jazz counted.

"Dear Moon, please use your mystical powers to help us make our dreams come true," the girls chanted, before throwing their pieces of paper towards the fire. A sudden breeze blew Portia's back into her face.

"That must be my parents trying to thwart me," she joked. "I told you they were evil." She threw the paper back into the fire and this time it was caught by one of the flames.

"This is going to sound crazy," Allegra said, "but now we've done that I actually feel like my dream's going to come true."

"Me too," said Jazz.

"Me three," said Hope with a smile.

"And me," said Portia.

High above them a wispy cloud drifted over the moon, dimming its light for a moment, before it re-emerged, brighter than ever.

Chapter Nineteen

Hope arrived home feeling strangely optimistic. She wasn't sure whether it was the sugar rush from the marshmallows and hot chocolate but it felt as though the glimmering moonlight had somehow worked its way into her. And yet it wasn't like the meeting had been a huge success. Allegra had been her usual annoying self, trying to make out that Hope's life hadn't been all that affected by her HCM, and Hope had made that terrible joke about Portia getting a life-threatening health condition, but at the end, when she'd had to burn her dream in the flames, she suddenly felt better and happier.

At first, she'd been so stumped for something to write she seriously considered making something random up, like, *I hate Allegra*. But then she'd been struck by a bolt of inspiration – she might not be able to wish away her HCM but she could try to wish away her fear. And so she'd written: *I dream of feeling less afraid.* Then, worried that it sounded a little weak, she'd added: *Please help me feel brave again.* Just the act of putting it into writing and then watching as her dream turned to fire, filled her with a new-found sense of hope. As she let herself into the house, she realized she hadn't once counted to three all the way home.

"There you are!" Petra exclaimed, hurrying into the hall to greet her. "We were worried about you."

Hope's spirits sank. "I'm only five minutes late."

"I know but…" Petra broke off but Hope could guess what she wanted to say. *We thought something bad had happened.*

Her optimism became tinged with Petra's fear. "Well, as you can see, I'm fine."

Petra gave a sigh of relief.

"I think I'm going to go to bed, get an early night."

"OK, goodnight." Petra hugged her tightly. Too tightly. Hope felt her mother's fear soak into her as if by osmosis. She trudged upstairs to her bedroom and sank onto her bed. What was the point in her dreaming of being happier and braver if her mum was going to infect her with fear every time she saw her? She went over to the window to look at the moon. But clouds had rolled in and all she could see was darkness.

Allegra left the seafront and walked up the road leading home. What she had just experienced was so different from a normal night with her normal friends that she needed a moment to take stock. She knew that if Chantelle and the others had seen her sitting round a fire burning her dreams, they would have had a field day. *What the hell are you freaks doing?* she imagined Chantelle saying in her lazy drawl. *Why are you, like, praying to the moon?* That's what it had felt like –

praying — as they'd all sat there watching their dreams ignite and curl up in flames. But unlike the monotonous Lord's Prayer that Magdalena had made her memorize when they still went to church, asking the moon for help making their dreams come true felt exciting and real. In the end Allegra had written two dreams on her piece of paper: *I wish I could visit Sofia.* And then, in a fit of desperation she'd added: *I wish I could end things with Alf without it causing an epic fallout.* For the first time since she'd realized she didn't actually like Alf all that much, she felt a slight sense of hope that maybe her dream could come true after all, even if she couldn't see exactly how to make it happen.

As she walked past a row of darkened shops closed for the night, she pondered how she might end things. She could tell Alf that her mum had forbidden her from seeing him. The irony made her smile. Magdalena seemed to think that the world revolved around romantic relationships. Nothing would make her happier than Allegra announcing she had a boyfriend. She'd probably want them to sit on the sofa doing each other's nails and comparing notes about Alf and Mr Straight Outta Cringeton. Still, Alf didn't know that. She walked past the kebab shop, the only shop still open, and breathed in the aroma of grilled meat. She was about to go in and buy a bag of chips when she saw a familiar figure lurking beneath the tree on the corner of her street. *What the hell?*

"Alf?" she called, striding towards him. "What are you doing?"

He stumbled towards her, veering off to the side. "'llegra, where you been?"

He sounded and looked drunk. Very drunk. All the optimism she'd been feeling vanished in an instant.

"Why are you here?" she asked, drawing level with him. His breath smelled of cigarettes and booze and his eyelids looked heavy.

"I needed to see you."

She felt hugely relieved that she'd never told him her exact address. "Where you been?" he asked again.

"I – uh – popped out to see my friend from my old dance class."

"Lying!" he exclaimed, staggering slightly.

"What?"

"Your mum said you were out with Chantelle. But I know you weren't 'cos Chantelle was down the park."

"You spoke to my mum!" *Crap! Crap! Crap!* "But you don't know my address."

"Chantelle gave it to me. Why did you tell your mum you were with us when you weren't?"

Think! Think! Think! "My mum – she never liked my friend Jazz, from my dance class…" *Yes, this was good…* "It was easier to lie to her and say I was with you lot than tell her the truth and get nagged to death. You didn't tell her I wasn't with Chantelle, did you?"

"Nah." He sighed heavily. "I thought…"

"What?"

"I thought you were with some other fella."

"Of course I wasn't." It was good to be able to say at least one thing that wasn't a lie.

"Good." He put his arm round her shoulder. It felt really heavy. "'Cos I – I like you, Leggy."

Oh god. She looked up through the branches of the tree, hoping to see the moon for some kind of inspiration but it seemed to have disappeared. "I like you too. But I'm going to have to get home or my mum's going to kill me."

"Your mum sounded pretty cool."

"Yeah, well... Hadn't you better get going too?"

He laughed. "My old man doesn't give a shit what time I get in." He stumbled slightly again and leaned into her. "He doesn't give a shit about anything."

"I'm really sorry," Allegra said, and she meant it.

"Yeah, well. Come on then, I'll walk you home."

"You don't have to."

"I want to."

His body was so heavy with drunkenness it felt more like Allegra was walking him as they stumbled arm in arm through the estate. Finally, they reached her block of flats.

"OK, goodnight then," she said, trying to disentangle herself.

"Don't I get a goodnight kiss?"

The last thing she wanted was his drunken mouth anywhere near hers but if it meant him leaving her in peace, it was a price worth paying. She closed her eyes and kissed him on the lips. His arms tightened around her and he clamped his mouth to hers. He tasted of sour alcohol. She felt as if she couldn't breathe.

"I've got to go," she gasped, pulling free.

"All right. See you tomorrow." He stared at her through unfocused eyes, then lurched away.

"Yes, see you." She quickly keyed the entry code into the pad by the main door and slipped inside. Now she had the time it took to climb the seven floors to her flat to come up with an explanation about who Alf was and why he'd been drinking, if her mum had been able to detect his drunkenness through the intercom, that is. By the time she reached her front door she'd decided to say he was a friend from school who had some issues.

She came in to find her mum sitting on the sofa in her satin robe, her hair scraped back in a bun and her face shiny with night cream.

"Hey, darling," she said, not looking up from her phone. "Nice night?"

"Yeah, thanks." Allegra held her breath and waited. The fact that Magdalena had called her darling was clearly a good sign. She never called her darling when she was annoyed with her. But surely she'd have something to say about Alf turning up. Allegra hadn't had a boy call for her before.

Magdalena giggled at something on her phone. "Jonny is such a sweetheart."

"Cool."

Magdalena kept on scrolling.

"I think I'm going to go to bed."

"OK, sweetheart. Sleep well." She still didn't look up.

Allegra turned to go.

"Oh, some boy called for you earlier."

Allegra stopped in the doorway.

"Said his name was Alf. He sounded lovely. Have you got something to tell me, darling? Have you met someone special too?" Magdalena finally glanced up and gave her a massive grin.

Allegra felt like wailing, *Why can't you be like a normal mum?* "No, he's just a friend from school."

"Ah, OK." She actually looked disappointed. "Goodnight, lovely," she said, looking back at her phone.

Portia decided to take the slightly longer route home, rather than cutting through the alleyway. This was partly for safety reasons, as it was now dark and her parents had drilled it into her not to go anywhere without streetlights when she was out on her own. But she also wanted the opportunity to do a bit of snooping, using the darkness as a cover. When she got to the front of the house where the dog lived, she stopped, pretending to do something on her phone but really glancing sideways at the house. She could see a thin chink of light coming from a gap in the curtains in one of the downstairs windows. After checking the street to make sure no one was coming, she crept up the path. If anyone came out of the house, she would pretend she had the wrong address. When she reached the front door, she took a couple of steps to the side and peered through the gap in the curtain.

"Holy cow!" she exclaimed. The gap might have been narrow but it was wide enough to see that the room was in a state of disarray. The part of the sofa that was visible was covered in old newspapers and other assorted litter and on the floor lay an upside-down plate with what looked like some kind of sauce or gravy seeping out from beneath it. Had the man thrown it in a fit of rage? Portia shivered. What if he'd thrown it at the dog? She heard a car purring up the road and stepped back into the shadow by the front door. As the car passed, there was a bark from inside the house. *Don't worry, little dog*, Portia said silently. *I'm going to save you if it's the last thing I do!*

Chapter Twenty

Jazz fumbled for her bleeping phone and turned off the alarm. She'd left her blinds open when she'd gone to bed the night before and the sunrise was painting the clouds tangerine and crimson. It looked epic.

"All right, let's do this!" she said, getting out of bed. After last night's Moonlight Dreamers meeting she'd decided to build on the momentum and have a stab at achieving her dream — to somehow learn to love paddleboarding — before she lost all enthusiasm again. She got into her wetsuit, wishing she was putting it on to go surfing, and glanced out at the water below. It was sheet calm. "Perfect weather for paddleboarding," she said sarcastically. She crept downstairs, careful not to wake her parents, and let herself out onto the deck.

The sunrise was so vivid it had even turned the ocean red. Jazz felt her resistance soften. It was good to be up and out at dawn again, and to be going out on the water, even if it would be in slow motion. She took her board and paddle from the cupboard at the end of the deck and made her way down to the beach, trying not to make too much noise on the pebbles. She didn't want to get Mikey's hopes up about the paddleboarding as she was still convinced she was going to hate it.

She carried her board to the water's edge. It felt weird carrying a board so much bigger than her surfboard. Weird and slightly awkward. She waded into the still water until it reached her waist, an old thrill building inside of her. It felt so great to be back in the water. She hadn't set foot in the ocean since arriving in the UK, partly due to her giant sulk at her parents and partly because the water was too cold for swimming. Now she couldn't help thinking she'd been her own worst enemy – a bit like the night in Brick Lane, when she'd missed out on all that delicious food. All this time she'd been feeling so homesick she hadn't realized that one of the places she felt most at home had been right outside her window all along!

Jazz stood still for a moment, letting the water lap at her body as if giving her welcoming kisses. Then she put her board fin down in the water and laid the paddle across it. She carefully placed one knee in the centre of the board and then the other. The board wobbled and for a moment she thought it was going to capsize but she shifted slightly and found the sweet spot. As she picked up the paddle, the nose of the board started tipping up. Damn, she was too far back. She quickly shifted forwards and the board steadied.

"OK, now to stand," she murmured to herself. Slowly and carefully, she stood, one foot at a time, being careful to stay in the middle of the board. Even though paddleboarding was like surfing for old people there was a strange familiarity about it. It still required complete focus in order to tune in to the ocean. She pushed the water with her paddle. A gentle wave rolled in, catching her board and sending it tipping. In a second, she was back in the water.

"Damn it!" she cried but she couldn't help laughing. It might be surfing for old people but it had still caught her out. She repositioned her board and prepared to climb on again.

Hope approached the bus stop, scanning the street for any sign of Allegra. Now she'd had the chance to sleep on it she realized she'd possibly been a little harsh last night. She'd thought Allegra was being dismissive of her HCM but maybe she was genuinely trying to be encouraging by getting Hope to focus on the things she could still do. She'd been hoping for the chance to see her on her own to try and clear the air but there was no sign of her. When the bus arrived, the seats in the third row were taken so she counted to three twice and sat down on the sixth. As the bus turned onto the road running parallel with the sea, she stared out of the window and thought back to the meeting the night before. It had felt so magical sitting around the fire in the moonlight. For a brief moment, anything had felt possible. If only she'd been able to bottle that feeling to take with her to school.

Hope's first lesson of the day was PE. Since the embarrassing incident in netball Ms Sykes had been really kind and told her that she could use the lesson time to do homework if she didn't want to join in. "The important thing is that you work out your own limits," she'd said. But now, buoyed up by last night's meeting, Hope was determined to confront her fear and show Allegra that she wasn't a wimp. She got to the changing rooms early and told Ms Sykes that she'd like to play goalkeeper.

"Are you sure?" Ms Sykes asked.

Hope nodded. "I'm allowed to do moderate exercise. I was just a little freaked out before. It was the first PE class since my diagnosis and I panicked."

"Of course," Ms Sykes replied. "It's bound to be a massive adjustment."

As Hope was changing, the rest of the class came trooping in. There was still no sign of Allegra and for a moment Hope thought she might be off sick. But then Allegra and her friend Chantelle hurried in, bringing with them a waft of perfume.

Allegra passed Hope and gave her the slightest nod. This was a good sign. Hope smiled back.

"Ah, there you are," Ms Sykes said to Allegra and Chantelle, as she came out of her office. "Allegra, Hope's going to be playing today so I've put her in as goalkeeper and moved you to goal defence."

This time, to Hope's relief, there was no moaning from Allegra.

"Of course," she said, smiling at Hope. Hope relaxed some more. Things looked promising.

"I'm going to set things up outside," Ms Sykes said. "Join me as soon as you're ready, girls."

"What is actually wrong with you, Hope?" Chantelle called across the changing room as soon as Ms Sykes had gone. The chatter from the other girls instantly hushed.

Hope swallowed hard before replying. "I – I have a heart condition."

The silence deepened.

For once, Chantelle looked lost for words, but only briefly. "Is it, like, terminal?"

"Chantelle!" Allegra exclaimed.

"What? I'm only asking."

"Yeah, but it's a bit personal."

Now all eyes were on Hope. She swallowed again, her mouth suddenly dry. "Hopefully not," she said quietly.

Thankfully, at that point, Ms Sykes came back into the room.

"I forgot the bibs," she said with a cheery grin. But Hope felt the stares of the other girls upon her and it made her skin crawl.

When they got out onto the court, she saw Chantelle saying something to Ms Sykes. Hope was too far away to hear but she could see Ms Sykes shaking her head. Hope glanced at Allegra, who had taken her position as goal defence. Her long legs were still tanned from the summer and her skin shone as if it had been polished. Allegra glanced over her shoulder and smiled at her again. As much as Hope was relieved that she was being more friendly, she couldn't help wondering if she could really trust her. How could someone who was best friends with Chantelle want to hang out with people like her, Jazz and Portia? It didn't make sense. Was she coming to the Moonlight Dreamers meetings as some kind of joke? Was she waiting to tell Chantelle all about them and ridicule her in front of everyone? As Hope felt her panic rising, she took a deep breath and tapped her leg three times.

Ms Sykes blew her whistle and the game began. This time when Hope saw the other team advancing towards her, she managed to keep her cool. One of the other team's players threw the ball high in the air to Chantelle, their goal shooter. Hope tried in vain to block it but even though it looked like an easy catch for Chantelle, she somehow managed not to get the ball. One of the girls on the other team shouted at Chantelle, "You didn't even try."

"Course I didn't," Chantelle yelled back. "I didn't want to give Hope a heart attack."

"But — you won't…" Hope muttered. She glanced at Allegra. She was staring at the ground.

The rest of the game followed exactly the same pattern. Any time the ball came near Chantelle and Hope, Chantelle made it patently obvious that she was backing away from the challenge. And any time Chantelle did get a shot on goal she seemed to deliberately miss. Hope ended up blocking six shots but she couldn't take any pleasure from it because she knew Chantelle wasn't trying.

Afterwards, Ms Sykes asked Hope to help her put away the balls and bibs.

"You played really well," she said and Hope felt a surge of pride. "How do you feel?"

"Really good," Hope replied. And it was true. In spite of Chantelle's antics she'd confronted her fear and played a whole game of netball and the worst hadn't happened. Her heart hadn't failed. And she'd proved to Allegra that she wasn't a coward.

But as soon as she got back to the changing room she knew something was wrong. Chantelle and her teammates were in a huddle by Allegra, talking in hushed tones. As Hope sat down on the bench across from them, they all turned to look at her.

"Do you really think it's fair, you doing PE?" Chantelle asked.

"What do you mean?" Hope's mouth went dry.

"Well, how are we supposed to play properly against you, when you could, like, have a heart attack any minute?"

"Chantelle!" Allegra snapped.

"What, Leggy? It's true. It was all right for you, you were playing on her team, but how is it fair for anyone who plays against her?" Chantelle sidled along her bench so that she was directly opposite Hope. "I know it must suck to be you but seriously, I don't think it's very fair to let it affect us, do you?"

"But it was only a practice session in a PE lesson," Hope said. "It's not as if we were playing in the league."

Chantelle gave an exaggerated sigh and pouted her glossy lips. "Yeah, but how are we supposed to practise properly when we're scared you might drop dead?"

Hope winced. It felt terrible hearing her worst fear being spat from Chantelle's mouth. She glanced at Allegra. She knew more about Hope's condition than Chantelle did. Maybe if she said something it would make a difference. But Allegra was staring into her lap as if she'd just discovered something really fascinating woven into her shorts.

"I'm all right playing goalkeeper as I don't have to do much running around."

"Yeah, but that wasn't even your position before, was it?" Chantelle pulled her top up and over her head, revealing a practically see-through black bra. "Leggy always played goalkeeper until you got ill."

"It's OK, I don't mind," Allegra said, so quietly her voice was barely more than a whisper.

"Yeah, you do," Chantelle snapped before looking back at Hope. "I think you should tell Ms Sykes you want to sit netball out, yeah?"

One...two...three...One...two...three... She wished she had the courage to tell Chantelle to shut up. She wished she had the courage to yell at Allegra for being so two-faced. But it was as if all of the eyes staring at her had somehow struck her dumb, so she sat there, like an idiot, nodding her head.

Chapter Twenty-One

"So who exactly were you out with last night?" Chantelle asked, staring at Allegra across the table in the school canteen. She'd reapplied her eyeliner after PE and it seemed to be exaggerating her stare. Allegra looked away to the line of year sevens streaming in through the door. They all looked so young and innocent in their crisp new uniforms and slightly oversized blazers. She thought back to two years ago, when she'd been just like them, scared of high school and desperate to make a friend. If only she hadn't been so desperate. If only Chantelle hadn't been the first girl to talk to her, things could have turned out so differently.

"I told you, a couple of girls I used to go to dance class with."

"What are their names?"

Geez, what was with the inquisition? Alf grilling her about where she'd been was bad enough; the last thing she needed was Chantelle joining in.

"Jazz and Portia."

"Ooh, sound posh." Chantelle's voice sharpened, the way it always did when she was picking on other students or talking about the teachers she hated. Allegra flinched as she remembered the conversation with Hope in the changing room. She'd so badly wanted to tell Chantelle to lay off, but Chantelle was already annoyed with her for not coming to the park last night. If she'd stuck up for Hope, she was afraid everything would start to unravel, and she didn't have the energy to deal with that right now. Hope drifted past their table. She looked so pale and tired, and so fed up. Allegra thought back to the meeting the night before, and how Hope had told them about her sister going off to uni. She'd seemed so sad about it, and after what Chantelle had just done she'd be feeling even worse. Allegra should have said something. Her whole body went hot with shame.

"I can't believe you chose to hang out with them instead of us," Chantelle continued. "We had a right laugh. Alf got so drunk — it was hilarious."

"Yeah, I saw him."

"What?" Chantelle's eyes narrowed. "When?"

"He was at the flats, waiting for me to get home."

Was it Allegra's imagination or did Chantelle look slightly disappointed?

"He was upset you never came," Chantelle said before taking a sip of her diet cola.

"Yeah, well, I'm sure he'll get over it." Allegra watched as Hope joined the queue for food. She needed to apologize to her, try and sort things out.

"What's wrong with you?" Chantelle scowled.

"What do you mean?"

"You're going out with Alf Beck — *Alf Beck*," she added in an exaggerated whisper. "Why are you being so cold to him?"

Now she had Allegra's full attention. "What do you mean, cold?"

"What you said just now, and…" she broke off.

"And?"

"Well, not letting him, you know…"

Allegra's stomach churned. "Not letting him what?"

"Get physical," Chantelle whispered across the table. A year seven student made the mistake of putting her tray down next to her. "Get lost," Chantelle hissed. The girl flushed red and practically ran from the table.

"How do you know what I've not let him do?"

Chantelle shrugged and looked away. "He told me, last night. He was upset, Leggy. He wanted to know if you'd said anything to me about it."

"Oh my god!"

"What?"

"I can't believe you were talking about me — about that."

"Why wouldn't I? I am your best mate."

But I don't want you to be. The sentence formed in Allegra's mind, in a moment of absolute clarity. Just as she didn't want Alf to be her boyfriend, she didn't want Chantelle, with her hard stare and spiteful tongue, to be her best friend. It was as if she were trapped in a nightmare life that didn't belong to her. She pushed her tray away. "I need some fresh air."

"Cool, let's go. I need a smoke." Chantelle put her uneaten plate of chips back on her tray.

"No. I — I've got to call my mum about something."

Chantelle's face pinched into a frown. "Oh. OK." Then she looked past Allegra and her frown melted into a smile as Alf and his friends entered the canteen. Allegra used to think that the way he swaggered was cool but now it just seemed cocky. Anger prickled at her skin. She couldn't believe he'd told Chantelle such a private thing about them.

"I'll see you later," she said, standing up and turning to go.

"All right, Leggy?" Alf called as she walked towards him.

"All right," she murmured in response.

He went to kiss her but she swerved her head away.

"Hey, what's up?" He looked concerned.

"I don't know. Why don't you ask Chantelle?" she snapped before marching past.

As soon as she got outside, she leaned against the wall and took a breath. Her heart was pounding. *What are you doing?* a voice squeaked inside her head. *Why are you trying to piss off your best friend AND your boyfriend?* She started walking on autopilot, wanting to get as far away from them as possible. She kept walking round to the front of the building and the main entrance. The gates stood in front of her, wide open, inviting. She carried on walking until she'd marched right through them.

Portia came out of Shirley's house and glanced next door, wondering if Jazz was back from school yet. While she'd been out walking Reggie she had formed the beginnings of a cunning plan and she could really do with Jazz's feedback. She hurried up the steps to Jazz's house and knocked on the door. A tanned woman with bobbed blonde hair answered.

"G'day," she said with a warm smile.

"Hello. Is Jazz home?"

"She is. Come in, I'll just give her a shout. Who shall I say it is?"

"Portia — her — uh — friend."

"Nice to meet you, Portia. I'm Cheryl, Jazz's mum. Jazz!" she called up the stairs. "There's a friend here for you."

"What?" Portia heard Jazz call back.

"Your friend Portia is here to see you."

"She'll be down soon." Cheryl smiled at Portia before disappearing into the kitchen. The next moment, Jazz came racing down the stairs, wearing the smart black-and-white uniform of Cedars College. It was strange to see her dressed so formally, it didn't look right.

"Hey!" Jazz cried and before Portia knew what was happening Jazz had flung her arms around her in a hug. Portia stood there stiff and slightly awkward, unsure what to do.

"I'm sorry!" Jazz laughed and let her go. "I'm just so pleased to see you."

"You are?" Portia wasn't sure anyone had ever said this to her before.

"Yes. When my mum said a friend was here to see me, I had to pinch myself."

"Why?"

"I thought I was dreaming." Jazz sighed. "I've had another crappy day at school. I tried chatting to this girl at lunchtime but then she said she needed to go to the toilet and she never came back. It's like I'm wearing some kind of friend-repellent. No one wants to have anything to do with me."

"Really?" Portia frowned. How could Jazz's schoolmates not like her? She was so friendly and so nice. Clearly Cedars students were even more stuck-up than she'd thought. "Just goes to show, money can't buy good taste."

Jazz laughed. "Thank you. So, are you on your way to walk Reggie? Do you want some company?"

"No – and yes. I've already walked the Regsta, but I would really like your company – and your advice."

"Sure. Hey, why don't we go up to my room and I'll get out of my prison scrubs." She grimaced and pulled her tie undone. "I can't believe I have to wear a skirt to school. I thought that kind of thing went out with the suffragettes."

"We get to choose whether we want to wear a skirt or trousers at my school," Portia replied. "I can't believe any girl would choose to wear a skirt, but maybe that's because I've grown up in a house full of boys. I have three brothers," she said as she followed Jazz into her bedroom. "Holy cow!" Portia gasped.

Practically all of the exterior wall was made of glass, and the view of the sea below was stunning. "This view is epic!"

"I know, right." Jazz went over to the window and looked out. "It took me a while to appreciate it because I was so homesick at first, but now I love it, especially at night when I can fall asleep listening to the waves."

"I bet." Portia joined her at the window. Jazz's house was at the end of the private road where the beach finished, a jagged crop of rocks forming a dividing line between it and the harbour next door. A man was sitting on the rocks, fishing. It was such a peaceful scene, and so different to the mayhem of the public beach.

"So, what was it you wanted my advice on?" Jazz asked, unbuttoning her shirt to reveal a white sports bra. Portia quickly looked back out at the sea.

"I've come up with a cunning plan to try and find out if that dog I was telling you about is being abused, but the trouble is I've come up with plans before that have gone a bit wrong – well, actually they've gone a *lot* wrong..."

"OK, so what is it?"

"Well, I was trying to think of an excuse to knock at the door, to try and figure out what the dog's owner is like, and I thought maybe I could pretend I was collecting for charity."

"Hmm..." Jazz slipped off her skirt and got into a pair of tracksuit bottoms.

Again, Portia averted her eyes. Clearly Jazz didn't have any body issues, unlike Portia, for whom getting changed in

PE was like performing an escape artist's routine, trying not to expose a centimetre of flesh. She'd never been bothered about nudity when she was younger but hitting puberty in a family of boys had made her suddenly self-conscious.

"I think coming up with an excuse to call at the house is a great idea," Jazz continued. "But I'm not so sure about the charity thing – unless it's genuine. What if he gave you some money? Or asked to see your ID? You could end up getting arrested for theft."

"See, this is exactly why I needed your opinion!" Portia exclaimed.

Jazz sat on her bed and Portia perched down beside her.

"I could pretend I was looking for someone else, and I'd got the wrong address."

"Yeah, but then the whole thing will be over in a couple of seconds." Jazz looked thoughtful for a moment. "I know, how about you pretend you're doing some kind of survey. That way you'll have a chance to ask them some questions."

"That's brilliant! You're a genius!"

Jazz laughed. "That's the first time I've been called that but thank you!"

"I could pretend I'm doing a survey about pets."

"Perfect!"

"I could ask him things like, how often he feeds his pet or takes it out for a walk."

Jazz nodded. "How about, on a scale of one to ten, how much do you love your dog?"

"Yes! Will you help me come up with some questions?"

"Of course." Jazz picked a laptop off the floor. "I can type them up and print them out if you like, make it look more professional."

Now Portia was the one who wanted to hug Jazz. She sat on her hands instead. "Let's do it!"

An hour later, the survey was complete and printed out. Jazz had had so much fun helping Portia come up with the questions she couldn't believe how dramatically her day had changed for the better, and she didn't want the fun to end.

"Do you want me to come with you?" she asked, crossing her fingers that Portia would say yes.

"Oh, would you?" Portia's brown eyes sparkled.

"Of course. I'll just tell the olds."

Jazz hurried into the kitchen where Cheryl was chopping a green pepper at the counter and Mikey was smoking a roll-up by the back door.

"Is it OK if I pop out with my friend for a bit? I won't be long."

"Have you made a friend at school?" Mikey asked hopefully.

"Er, I think there's more chance of me making my bed than making a friend in that place," Jazz replied.

"Wow, is it that bad?" Mikey whistled through his teeth.

Jazz gave a grim smile. "I've made friends with the girl who walks the dog next door, her name's Portia."

"She looks really nice," Cheryl said. "Where are you off to?"

"Just helping her do a survey thing. I won't be long."

Jazz hurried back to Portia, who was waiting in the hall. "Let the cunning plan begin," she said with a grin.

Outside, the sun was beginning its descent over the ocean, streaking the sky lilac and pink. As the girls hurried along the seafront, Jazz glanced at the water. "So, I finally took my paddleboard out this morning."

"Really? How was it?"

"Not as bad as I was expecting." Jazz laughed. "I mean, nothing will ever beat surfing but it felt good to be back in the water."

"I bet. Well done." Portia smiled at her. "I'm so glad you started this Moonlight Dreamers thing."

"Really?" Jazz's happiness grew.

"Yeah. It's good to have something that makes you chase after your dreams, otherwise you just drift through life, don't you? Kind of like a paddleboard."

Jazz chuckled. "Yes, exactly." She sighed. "I just wish our other members liked each other a little better."

"Yeah," Portia agreed. "Things are definitely still a little tense. I did feel sorry for Allegra when Hope bit her head off for telling her she could still have dreams – although it must be so hard for Hope having a heart condition.

"Absolutely." Jazz made a mental note to reach out to Hope and see how she was doing.

When they got close to the old pier, Portia led them across the road and up one of the streets leading into town.

"Let's cut through here," she said after a few minutes, pointing to an alleyway. It was lined with walls and gates backing onto a row of houses. The walls were dotted with graffiti tags and stickers advertising clubs. Jazz grinned. As much as she liked living down by the beach, it was fun to visit the buzzing heart of Brighton.

"This is where the dog lives," Portia whispered, coming to a halt by an old wooden gate and peering through the gap. "No sign of the dog in the garden," she reported. Portia stepped back and Jazz had a look, noticing a patchy lawn.

"Let's go and do our questionnaire," Portia said.

The front of the house looked as forlorn as the back. Jazz wondered what kind of person would be living there. She thought of what Portia had said before and pictured a large, shaven-headed man, arms covered in tattoos and she shivered, both from fear and excitement. After weeks of feeling so flat and depressed it was great to be having an adventure.

"Ready?" Portia asked.

"Ready," Jazz replied.

They went up the path and Portia knocked on the door. From deep inside the house came the sound of a dog barking. It was the kind of high-pitched yelp belonging to a small dog, like a terrier.

Jazz leaned closer to the frosted-glass panel in the centre

of the door. "Maybe the owner's out." But then she saw a shadowy figure. "I just saw someone," she whispered.

Portia knocked on the door again, louder this time. But there was no more movement. The dog's barking became increasingly frantic, and then suddenly there was silence.

"Oh no. You don't think he hit the dog, do you?" Portia's eyes widened. She crouched down, lifted the letterbox and peered inside. "Look!"

Jazz scanned the road to make sure no one was watching, then bent to look too. It took a moment for her eyes to adjust to the gloom inside but slowly she noticed a pile of leaflets and letters on the floor, fanning out from the door.

"Wow," she whispered.

Portia knocked again but now Jazz wasn't so sure this was the right thing to do. Whoever was inside was clearly avoiding them. "I think maybe we need a new plan," she whispered, feeling suddenly uneasy. To her relief, Portia nodded.

"You're right. It's time for action. That dog needs rescuing."

Chapter Twenty-Two

Dear Abuela... Allegra stopped typing and thought for a moment. If she wrote how she was really feeling, Sofia would worry, so she needed to keep things as light as possible. *I hope all is well up in the mountains. All is good here. Well, apart from the fact that I hate Mama, and I'm starting to hate my best friend and I don't want to go out with my boyfriend any more.* Allegra sighed and pressed DELETE. *Dear Abuela, I really miss you. I wish I'd come to see you this summer. I was thinking – maybe I could visit during my half-term holiday next month instead. It would be so nice to spend some time with you and drink that amazing fresh mint tea in the Sufi café and taste your incredible tapas and paella.* OK, this was good. And it might help make her dream of going to Spain come true. She only hoped she hadn't hurt Sofia's feelings too badly by turning down her invitation to come and stay in the summer. *Hoping to hear from you soon. Lots of love, Allegra xxxx*

She pressed SEND and went over to her bedroom window. After walking out of school on Friday she'd told Magdalena she'd got the flu and had extended her fake illness right through the weekend, then been given today off sick. Having a mum who didn't care about your education – even when she knew you were probably faking an illness – had some bonuses. Magdalena never minded phoning in sick for her. And now Allegra had some much-needed breathing space.

Both Chantelle and Alf had texted her Friday night, wondering where she'd disappeared to and Allegra had used the flu excuse on them too. But she was painfully aware she'd only put her problems on hold. The feeling that she'd suddenly woken up in the wrong life still haunted her. But how could she find the right life? What *was* the right life for her? An image of her and the other Moonlight Dreamers sitting on the beach the other night popped into her head. In spite of the randomness of sitting round a fire with a group of virtual strangers, it had felt so right. *Maybe you don't know how wrong something is until you find the right thing*, she thought to herself.

Jazz logged on to the school computer and started to type.

G'day, Hope,

How are you? Hope you had a great weekend. I am writing to you from my school library. Turns out this is where all the waif and stray kids hang out at lunchtime. I never set foot in my school library back at home – apart from when we had to for English. But I couldn't face being blanked by my fellow schoolmates in the canteen again. And turns out the library isn't so bad after all. So far this lunchtime I've started reading a book about great white sharks – did you know they have 300 teeth?! Seven rows of them apparently!!! I assume there aren't any great whites off the coast of Brighton? I hope not 'cos guess what! I went out on my paddleboard yesterday morning, and it wasn't as boring as I thought it would be. I saw an epic sunrise too. Anyway, how are you? I was wondering if you'd like to come and hang out at mine this evening after school? No worries if you already have something planned – I'm getting very used to my own company! Anyway, I hope you're having a good day.

Jazz xx

Dear Jazz,

Guess what! I'm in my school library too! I actually just volunteered to be a library monitor plus books are my thing so it was already my favourite place in the school. I'd love to hang out with you this evening, thank you! And I'm really sorry you're still having a tough time at your new school. But if it's any consolation, I think you'll discover that the most interesting people tend to hang out in the library. ☺

I'll be going to the café straight from school so just let me know what time you'd like me to come over – and if you'd like me to bring doughnuts???

Hope xx

Dear Hope,

BRING DOUGHNUTS!!! How about 5 p.m.? You can stay for dinner too. My dad's bound to be grilling something. Really looking forward to seeing you.

Jazz xx

As Hope set off along the seafront to Jazz's house, she felt something strangely close to happiness growing inside her. She didn't want to tempt fate but today had actually been a good day. Firstly, Allegra had been off sick, and Chantelle seemed way too preoccupied with her own dramas to bother Hope. And then, when Hope had gone to see the school librarian, Ms Doyle, about spending her PE lessons in the library doing homework, Ms Doyle had asked her if she'd like to become a library monitor.

"I think you'd do a great job," she'd said with a smile. "For a start you must have read every book in stock so you'd be great at giving students reading recommendations, and it's always good to have something like this on your CV."

The more Hope thought about becoming a library monitor, the happier it made her. Before, when she went to the library at break-times, it was like taking refuge, but now she would have a purpose. She thought about the email Jazz had sent earlier. It seemed crazy that someone as nice as Jazz should be frozen out by her fellow students but Hope knew only too well how cruel people could be. And it must be so hard trying to fit in when you come from another country. Once she reached Jazz's road and walked past the assorted sports cars and four-by-fours gleaming in the sunshine, she saw Jazz bouncing a basketball on the ground outside her house. As soon as she saw Hope, she stopped bouncing and grinned.

"Hope! How's it going?"

"Good. How are you?"

Jazz smiled. "Much better now I'm home from school. Thanks so much for coming round."

"Thank you for inviting me." Hope felt suddenly self-conscious. She hoped she and Jazz would get on OK without the other girls there to fill any awkward silences. She followed Jazz up the steps and into the house, catching a waft of incense. An electric guitar was propped against the wall in the corner of the hall, next to some kind of amp.

"Is that yours?" she asked, trying to make conversation.

Jazz laughed. "No. It's my dad's. He's a music producer."

"Oh, right." So that explained how they could afford to live in a house like this and send Jazz to Cedars College.

Jazz led her into the kitchen, which looked out on to the sea.

"It feels like being on a boat," Hope laughed as she looked at the waves outside the window.

"I know, right! You should see what it's like when the tide comes right in. The other night when it was windy, I thought the waves were going to hit the window!" Jazz opened the huge American-style fridge and took out a carton of orange juice. "What flavours did you get?" she asked, eyeing Hope's takeaway box of doughnuts hungrily.

"Strawberries and cream, raspberry ripple and chocolate lime," Hope replied.

"Awesome!"

They went over to a table by the window and sat on the bench.

"So Portia and I went on an undercover op on Friday," Jazz said, pouring them both a glass of juice. "To that house with the dog."

As Jazz filled Hope in on the rundown state of the house and how she'd thought at one point they were going to be abducted, Hope could barely believe her luck. It felt so nice to be hanging out with a friend after school like this. So normal.

"Portia's talking about us mounting some kind of rescue attempt," Jazz said.

"*What*? How?"

"Don't ask me. I think she's going to tell us at the meeting on Thursday."

A silence fell and Hope scrambled to think of something to say. She so badly wanted this to go right, for Jazz not to think her boring. She could sense the bud of a friendship forming between them but it was so delicate it could easily be squashed. Then she remembered the email Jazz had sent.

"So, you went out on your paddleboard?"

"Yeah." Jazz looked out at the sea, which was as flat and still as a lake. "I have to admit, it was kind of soothing."

"I bet."

"Have you ever done it before?"

Hope shook her head. Jazz looked thoughtful for a moment. "If you like, I could take you for a ride right now?"

"How do you mean?"

"You could sit on the front of the board and I could paddle. It's so still out there I'm sure we'll be fine."

"Oh…" A plague of *what ifs* started buzzing around Hope's head. *What if the board capsized? What if she needed to swim? What if it put too much pressure on her heart?*

"You're able to swim, right?"

"Yeah, but…"

"Not that I'd go out that far."

"I'm not sure…"

Hope detected the briefest flicker of disappointment on Jazz's face.

"No worries. I just thought…" Jazz looked back at the sea. "I'd been resisting paddleboarding for so long but it made me feel so much better being out on the water. It's like something magical takes over. It's hard to explain. I thought it might help you too. And you wouldn't have to do anything – just sit on the board and enjoy the view."

Hope tapped her leg under the table. *One… two… three…* She tapped her other leg. *One… two… three…* She really didn't want to go out on the water. But she really didn't want to disappoint Jazz either and, on balance, disappointing Jazz was the worst option. "OK," she said quietly.

The next few minutes passed by in a daze, as Hope and Jazz got changed into wetsuits. Unfortunately, Jazz had several so Hope wasn't able to use the excuse that she had nothing to wear. Then before she knew it, they were crunching along the beach towards the water, Jazz holding the huge board and Hope clutching the paddle. The sea was calm and still and several other people were out on their boards and no one appeared to be falling off.

"OK, getting on is the trickiest bit," Jazz said as they began wading out into the water. Thankfully, in the wetsuit it didn't feel cold at all. Jazz held the board flat on the water between them. "I'll hold it steady so you can climb on, then I'll get on behind you," she said.

Hope felt her pulse quicken as she grabbed the board and then, as instructed by Jazz, she placed one knee on top and then the other.

"That's it," Jazz cried. "You've done it."

Jazz got on behind her and the board lurched to the right, tipping them both back into the water. Hope gasped as a salty wave lapped at her face. Jazz giggled. "How about we both try and get on at the same time?"

"Sure." Now that Hope had fallen off the board and lived to tell the tale it didn't seem quite so scary. If anything, falling off had felt invigorating.

"OK." Jazz stood behind Hope. "One, two, three…" This time was a complete disaster and the board went flying out from under them.

"Oh the shame!" Jazz giggled. "I think this is the first time I've been glad to be seventeen thousand kilometres from home, so no one I know can see me!"

"I can see you," Hope giggled.

"Yeah, but you're just as useless as me so it doesn't count."

The more they tried, the harder it seemed, and the more they dissolved into hysterical laughter.

"I think I might wet myself," Hope cried, clutching her side.

"Not in my wetsuit, you don't," Jazz said, brandishing the paddle at her.

After what seemed like for ever both girls finally managed to climb on and stay on.

"Yes!" Jazz exclaimed. "We did it!"

Hope heard the sound of the paddle splashing and slowly they started to glide through the water. She sat cross-legged at the front of the board and drank in the view. Before her diagnosis she and Megan had gone swimming in the sea every summer, pretending to be mermaids named Allura and Neptuna, for whom Hope created dramatic and suspenseful adventures. This was the first year Hope hadn't been. After her diagnosis she'd been afraid that if a sudden current caught her, trying to swim against it would be too strenuous for her heart. But being on the board with Jazz felt safe, and it had been so much fun.

"I haven't laughed that much in ages," she said, looking across the water towards the ruins of the old pier.

"Me neither," Jazz replied. "It felt great, didn't it? What the hell!" she exclaimed. "Check out those birds!"

Hope glanced up to see a huge flock of starlings flying towards the sea, swirling together in perfect formation.

"How are they all flying together like that?" Jazz asked.

"It's called a murmuration," Hope replied. "They do it every evening during autumn and winter before they go to sleep. They roost on the old pier," she explained.

"I've never seen anything like it," Jazz gasped. "It's so beautiful."

"I know." Hope stared up at the birds, swooping and soaring, soaring and swooping, and all of a sudden her eyes filled with tears. *I don't want to live in constant fear of dying,* she thought to herself in a moment of total clarity. *I want to make friends and laugh till my sides ache and have dreams and watch the birds soar and gaze at the sea. I want to live my life to the fullest.*

Chapter Twenty-Three

Allegra's week crawled on, like a slow-motion montage of daytime TV, grazing the kitchen cupboards, staring at her bedroom ceiling and scrolling social media, until finally, it was Thursday. She'd been worried that, having taken the week off with "flu", there would be no way Magdalena would allow her to go out for the Moonlight Dreamers meeting, but it turned out that Magdalena had a date with Jonny.

"He won't tell me where he's taking me," she gushed as the microwave pinged and she took out a ready meal. "He's so romantic."

"Cool," Allegra replied, watching as Magdalena scooped a lasagne from its plastic tray onto a plate and put it on the table in front of her. "Thanks."

"I don't know what time I'll be home but it'll be late." Magdalena took a bottle of pinot from the fridge and poured herself a glass.

"That's great – I mean fine." Allegra was so relieved she could barely contain herself. She would be out and back without Magdalena knowing she'd ever left the flat.

"Ah, thanks for being so understanding, honey."

Magdalena planted a kiss on top of her head and Allegra caught a waft of her Chanel perfume – the one she wore on very special occasions. She felt a wistful pang at the thought of her mum going to so much effort for a creep like Jonny, but at least she'd now be able to go to the Moonlight Dreamers meeting. And she really needed to.

Sofia hadn't replied to her email, so she must have been hurt by Allegra not coming for the summer. Her abuela had been known to hold a grudge for years. Once, when the village priest cut her off in traffic, she didn't go to confession for almost a year. "Why should I confess my sins to someone who expects other cars to part for him, like Moses parting the Red Sea?" she'd said to anyone who'd listen. The thought of having offended Sofia was horrible. It was as if Allegra had lost her last true ally in the world. The Moonlight Dreamers was her only hope.

As soon as Magdalena had left for her date, Allegra scrambled out of the dressing gown she'd been living in for the past week and had a quick shower. Then she put on a dress Sofia had bought her the last time she visited Spain, a wrap-around in a beautiful shade of jade. Allegra paired it with black opaque tights and a pair of black patent DMs. Looking in the mirror she felt a little better. She loved how just the right outfit could make her feel exactly how she wanted, like a prescription in clothing form. Her DMs made her strong, and the dress from her abuela brought her comfort. She couldn't understand why some people didn't view clothes in this way, and would pull on any old thing. They were really missing out.

She ran down the stairs of her block of flats and into the dusk outside. A couple of kids were kicking a football against the bins and the old man who lived on the ground floor was walking his dog. Allegra smiled. It felt good to be outside again after her self-imposed quarantine. But then she saw someone walking towards her, someone with an instantly recognizable swagger.

"Alf!"

"All right, Leggy? I was just coming to see you." He looked her up and down, taking in her figure-hugging dress and shiny boots. "I thought you were sick."

"I was. I am. But I'm starting to feel a bit better." She hoped he wasn't able to see her face flushing in the twilight.

"Where are you off to?"

Her initial shock and embarrassment began to fade, replaced by anger. What was he doing here again, checking up on her?

"Just popping round to see a mate."

"Chantelle and that lot are down the park."

"I'm not going to see them."

"Oh." He stuffed his hands in his tracksuit pockets, looking dejected. "Who are you going to see then?"

"My friend Jazz, from my old dance class." She started walking down the road.

"Why are you pissed off?" he asked, running alongside her.

"I'm not. I just don't get why you keep turning up here uninvited."

"Uninvited? I'm your boyfriend – aren't I?"

She stopped walking and looked at him. "Maybe we…"

"What?" His expression hardened.

"Maybe we made a mistake."

"What do you mean?"

"Being boyfriend and girlfriend. Maybe we should just be friends." Her heart began to thud. But, much as she was nervous at how he might react, she knew she was doing the right thing.

"Are you dumping me?"

"We only started going out a couple of weeks ago."

He laughed incredulously. "I can't believe *you're* dumping *me*."

There was something so arrogant about the way he said this that Allegra instantly saw red. "And that is exactly the problem," she snapped.

"What are you talking about?"

She strode on, all of her anger at Alf and Magdalena and her stupid mid-life-crisis boyfriend swirling, hot and sour, in the pit of her stomach. But most of all she was angry at herself. How could she have put a boy she barely knew before her beloved abuela?

"You can't believe I'm dumping you because you're too arrogant to see things from my point of view." She stopped again and glared at him. "Have you ever asked me a single question about myself? Have you got a clue what's going on in my life right now? Are you even remotely interested? All you do is talk about yourself. How can that not be boring to me?"

"What the hell?" Anger sparked in his eyes, an anger she hadn't seen in him before. She swallowed hard and carried on walking.

"Yeah, well, maybe I haven't asked you anything 'cos I find *you* boring," he called after her.

"Really?" she called without looking back, trying to ignore how much his words stung.

"Yeah, you don't even let me touch you."

She stopped dead. "Well why don't you go and cry to Chantelle about it?"

For a split second he actually looked hurt. "Chantelle?"

"Yeah, like you did the other day when you moaned to her. Do you really think I'd be intimate with someone who blabs about it to everybody?"

His face fell. "Why are you being such a bitch?"

"I'm not being a bitch. I'm just being honest." She turned and carried on walking, hot tears burning in her eyes. She marched all the way to the seafront and it was only then that she stopped and looked over her shoulder. Thankfully, he was gone.

"I have a cunning plan," Portia announced. "And I need your help." She looked around the fire hopefully at the other girls.

"Is this to do with the dog?" Jazz asked.

"Yes. I now have almost conclusive proof that the dog is being mistreated."

"*Almost* conclusive?" Hope asked.

Although Portia was glad Hope was opening up more, she didn't appreciate any attempts to undermine her plan. "Yes. When I walked past the house this afternoon, the dog was in the back garden, scratching at the back door to be let in."

"Maybe the owner had popped out for a while," Hope suggested.

Portia sighed. Why, oh why did Hope suddenly have to become talkative now? "Yes, but when I left three hours later to come here, it was still trying to get in."

"Maybe the owner's gone out for the evening," Hope said.

"Or maybe the owner just doesn't care." Portia looked at Jazz for help. "Jazz, you saw the state of the house when we did our undercover op. Didn't it look like the type of house that might belong to an animal abuser?"

"Undercover op?" Allegra echoed. It was pretty much the first thing she'd said since she'd got to the meeting, Portia noted. And she'd been looking really distracted.

"Yes, we called round pretending to be doing a survey," Portia replied.

Allegra arched her perfectly defined eyebrows. "Did anyone answer?"

"No, but someone was home – we saw their shadow in the hall."

"It was seriously creepy," Jazz said with a shiver. "Hot chocolate?" She passed the flask to Hope.

"So, what's your cunning plan?" Hope asked as she poured herself a drink.

"I'm going to climb into the garden and rescue it," Portia said defiantly.

"When?" Allegra asked.

"Well, I was hoping tonight." Portia looked into the flames, not daring to meet the other girls' gazes. They were bound to try and talk her out of it.

"But where will you take it?" Hope asked.

"Back home. I'll tell my parents I found it wandering the streets."

"But what if you get caught?" Jazz asked.

"That's why I need your help – to be my lookout – or call the police if the owner tries to kidnap me – or worse." Portia glanced up, worried she might have overdone it. But the others were looking at her intently. It was time to play her trump card. "Isn't one of the rules of being a Moonlight Dreamer that we help each other in the pursuit of our dreams?"

"I guess we could go and have a look, try and suss things out." Jazz glanced at the others. To Portia's surprise, Hope was nodding. Only Allegra looked undecided. "OK," Jazz said, getting to her feet. "I'll tell my parents we're popping out to get some chips. I'll meet you guys out front."

All the way back through town, Portia became increasingly nervous. What if the dog had been taken inside?

What if it was still outside but the owner caught her trying to rescue it? What if she got her new friends into trouble? Allegra, for one, looked reluctant to be there, walking along silently and staring at the ground as Hope and Jazz talked about paddleboarding.

"Here we are," Portia said quietly when they reached the alleyway. The other girls stopped talking as Portia led them down towards the house. She peered through the crack by the gate. At first it was too dark to see anything but then she noticed a blur of white move across the grass.

"Hello, mate," she whispered as the dog scampered over, whimpering.

"Oh wow, it must have been outside for ages," Jazz said quietly.

"Yep," Portia agreed. "Right, can one of you give me a leg-up so I can get over?"

"Sure." Jazz linked her hands, palms up, for Portia to step into.

"Wish me luck." Portia smiled anxiously.

"Be careful," Hope whispered, tapping her fingers on the wall.

"Good luck," Jazz and Allegra murmured.

Portia lifted herself up onto the top of the wall and the dog started barking. Thankfully the house next door was completely dark. She took one of Reggie's treats from her jacket pocket and threw it into the garden. It did the trick and the dog started munching away – it must have been starving, poor thing. Portia dropped down into the garden and a security light above the back door came on. Typical, why didn't it come on when the dog moved around? She pressed herself into the shadows by the wall and waited for it to go off.

"Are you OK?" Jazz whispered from the alleyway.

"Yeah. I'm just going to get one of the garden chairs to stand on, so I can pass the dog over to you."

"Cool," Jazz replied.

"Take care," Hope whispered.

Portia gave the dog another treat and bent down to pat him. "Poor thing," she whispered. "Don't worry. I'm going to save you." Staying close to the fence, she made her way up and onto what was left of the patio. The slabs were uneven with clusters of weeds springing through the cracks. As she crept over to get one of the rusty chairs, she noticed a flickering light coming through one of the windows. At first she thought it was a candle, but as she crept closer and pressed her face to the glass she realized that it was the gas hob. There was no pan on top, though. Weird. Portia peered further into the gloom.

Dishes were piled in the sink and what looked like a rolled-up blanket was on the floor – or was it... She took a step back, almost treading on the dog who was now whimpering at her ankles.

"It's OK," she whispered, her voice trembling. She took her phone from her pocket and turned on the torch, her hands shaking as she held the light up to the window. "Oh no!" she gasped as she looked inside.

"Portia, are you OK?" Jazz hissed from the other side of the wall.

Portia raced back down the garden, the dog at her heels. "Inside the house," she gasped through the crack by the gate. "There's a body on the floor!"

Chapter Twenty-Four

For a moment it was as if everything had stopped, including Jazz's heart. Maybe she'd listened to too many true crime podcasts but when people talked about seeing a "body", there was usually the word "dead" in front of it.

"What do you mean, a body?" she hissed through the gap by the gate.

"Exactly that," Portia replied. "At first I thought it was a pile of clothes or a blanket but then I shone my torch on it."

Peering through the crack, Jazz could see Portia's eyes staring at her in the darkness, wide with fright.

"Where is it?" Jazz asked.

"In the kitchen. I noticed that one of the burners on the hob was on so I had a quick look inside and that's when I saw it."

"Do you think – do you think whoever it is is dead?" Jazz asked, the skin on her arms erupting in goosebumps.

"I don't know. They weren't moving at all, not even when I shone the torch on them."

"Crap!" Jazz glanced at Hope and Allegra, who both looked as scared as she felt. "What should we do?"

"Portia, are you able to climb back over?" Hope asked.

There was a scrambling sound from the other side of the wall and the dog started to whimper. "No, there's a steeper drop this side and the chair isn't high enough."

"Oh no." Jazz wracked her brains. She was pretty sure Amber had never had to deal with discovering a dead body in her Moonlight Dreamer days – there definitely wasn't a rule about what to do if you found one.

"Is there any way one of you could climb over?" Portia said, her voice trembling. "I'm getting a little freaked out being here on my own."

"I'll do it," Allegra said.

"Thank you!" Portia exclaimed.

"Maybe we should all climb over. Safety in numbers?" Jazz suggested. She looked at Hope.

"Yes, let's," Hope replied. "Then we can call for help once we know what's going on."

"Good plan," Jazz said. "OK, I'll give you guys a leg-up and then I'm pretty sure I can get over on my own." She helped Hope, then Allegra, then scrambled over the wall herself.

The little dog sniffed at her legs and she bent down to pet him. "It's all right, mate, we're going to fix this," she said, sounding a lot more confident than she felt. She glanced over the fence at the house next door. It was completely dark. "OK, let's have a look," she whispered.

The four of them crept up to the house. As they drew closer, the security light flicked on again, bathing them in harsh white light. It reminded Jazz of an old prison break movie her dad liked, although they weren't trying to escape, they were walking right towards potential danger. *Well, you did want something to happen in your life*, she told herself, fighting the sudden and completely inappropriate urge to laugh hysterically. Next to her, she heard Hope mutter something under her breath. It sounded like she was counting.

"Look," Portia whispered, going over to the window.

They peered inside. The flame was still burning on the hob, then Jazz's throat tightened. Portia was right, there was a body. She could just make out a pale hand sticking out, completely motionless.

"Do you think…" Allegra whispered. "Do you think they're dead?"

Jazz gulped.

"I think we should call the emergency services," Hope said.

"Yes." Jazz took out her phone. Her fingers were shaking so much she almost dropped it.

"I've never seen a dead body before," Portia whispered.

And then suddenly, the hand twitched.

"Oh my god!" Allegra exclaimed.

"It's come back to life!" Portia cried.

"Er, maybe it was never dead?" Jazz took a deep breath and tried to calm herself. "We should try and get in."

Portia looked up. "That upstairs window's open. I could scale up the drainpipe and climb in."

"Calm down, Spider-Man," Jazz replied. "We don't want to have to get an ambulance for you too!" She pushed down on the door handle. "It's unlocked!" As she opened the door, the little dog flew past her into the house, barking loudly.

Jazz turned to the others. "Come on."

The kitchen was really warm. Hope went straight to the cooker and turned off the hob. Jazz crept over to the door and felt for a switch. She clicked it on and the room was flooded with light. There was a gasp from the floor. An elderly woman was lying on her side, wisps of long white hair falling over her face.

Jazz crouched down beside her. "Are you all right?"

The woman looked up, fearful.

"It's OK, we're here to help," Jazz said gently.

The dog scampered around the woman, licking her face.

"Fell..." she whispered through cracked lips.

"Do you want some water?" Jazz asked.

She nodded.

"Should we call an ambulance?" Hope asked.

"Yeah. I'll do it," Allegra replied. "What's the address?"

As Portia told Allegra the address, Jazz took off her jacket and put it over the woman's trembling body. "My name's Jazz," she said. "We came into your garden because we heard your dog barking and we wanted to check everything was OK."

"Thank you," the woman whispered.

Hope came over with a glass of water. Very slowly and gently, Jazz lifted the woman's head and Hope held the glass to her lips.

"It's OK. You're going to be OK," Hope whispered.

The woman took a sip.

Allegra came back into the room. "They're sending an ambulance but they said it might take a while."

"Maybe we should try and make her a bit more comfortable," Hope suggested.

"Good plan." Jazz looked at the woman. "Would it be OK if we got you a blanket and some pillows?"

"Yes. Bedroom … upstairs…" the woman stammered.

"I'll go," Allegra said.

"I'll come with you," said Hope.

Hope followed Allegra out of the kitchen into the hallway. As her eyes adjusted to the darkness, she saw that the carpet by the front door was covered in letters, flyers and free papers.

"How long do you think she's been lying there?" Hope whispered as they went upstairs.

"I don't know. I hope she's going to be OK," Allegra replied.

"Me too." It was strange, but seeing the old woman so helpless and vulnerable on the floor seemed to have put a different filter on everything, making Hope's falling-out with Allegra seem so trivial in comparison.

"I don't want her to die." Allegra stopped on the landing and turned to look at Hope. Her eyes were shiny with tears.

"I'm sure she won't."

"But she looks so…"

Allegra seemed really different today, so on edge. Hope

wondered if it was connected to the fact that she hadn't been in school since Friday.

"She made me think of my abuela," Allegra continued.

"Your grandma in Spain?" Hope asked, remembering Allegra speaking about her at the last meeting.

Allegra nodded. "I don't want her to die," she said again, and Hope wasn't sure if she was talking about her grandma or the woman downstairs. Maybe she was talking about both.

"She's not going to die," Hope said firmly. "Because we're going to save her."

"Yes." Allegra looked at the doors leading off the landing. "Which do you think is the bedroom?"

"How about this one?" Hope nudged the door closest to her. It opened on to a bathroom. A smell of lavender wafted out.

Allegra opened the next door and turned on the light. A large double bed covered in a pink satin quilt took up most of the room. On one side was a small chest of drawers displaying a silver-framed photo of an elderly couple. They had to be in their seventies at least, each with an arm around the other, gazing adoringly into each other's eyes. They reminded Hope of her parents, but because they weren't her parents their display of affection was touching rather than annoying. The woman looked so happy and healthy too, her hair piled into a bun, her lips pursed like a rosebud.

"Do you think that was her?" Allegra whispered, pointing

to a large framed photo on the wall. It was a black-and-white portrait of a ballerina, mid-pirouette.

"Maybe." Hope glanced back at the bed. A book titled *Choreography and Dance Theatre* was open on the quilt. She gulped. It was hard to believe the same woman was lying helpless and immobile on the floor downstairs. "Come on," she said, pulling the quilt from the bed.

Allegra grabbed a couple of pillows and they hurried downstairs, back to the kitchen. Hope was relieved to see that the woman was now sitting up, propped against the cooker, with Jazz and Portia sitting either side of her.

"Here you are," she said, gently placing the quilt over her.

"Oh, you are a dear, thank you." The woman's voice was stronger now. Hope thought she could detect a slight accent but she wasn't sure where from. "I'm so sorry for causing all of this drama."

"Don't be silly," Jazz said. "You couldn't help falling over."

"It's my hip. It's been giving me so much trouble. The doctors want to replace it but I don't know what I'd do with my poor dear Nurey if I went into hospital."

The dog ran over and jumped into the woman's lap. "Oh, Nurey, you were outside for so long," she said, stroking his head.

Hope glanced at Portia. How could she have thought the dog was being abused? Clearly he was well loved by his owner, and adored her too, judging by the way he kept licking her face.

"Do you live here alone?" Portia asked.

"Yes, since my husband died three years ago."

"I live in the next street," Portia said. "I thought I saw a man here last week – a big man with cropped hair."

The woman frowned for a moment before a flicker of recognition passed across her face. "Oh, you must have seen Roger – my husband's son from his first marriage. He comes round every so often to see how I'm doing, pestering me to go and look at care homes, prepare for the future. I think he just wants me out of the way so he can do the place up." She grimaced. "You don't think they'll put me in a home because I fell, do you? I couldn't bear it. All they do in those places is sit around in armchairs doing crossword puzzles. I hate crossword puzzles."

"Me too!" said Jazz.

The woman smiled at her. "What's your name, dear?"

"Jazz – short for Jasmine. No one ever calls me that – apart from teachers."

The woman chuckled. "I like Jazz – it has spirit. I'm Raissa. And who are you?" She looked at the others.

As the girls introduced themselves, Hope glanced around the kitchen. The appliances were a little old but the room was clean and tidy. There were two bowls by the back door. One of them had WORLD'S CUTEST DOG printed around the rim. How had Portia got it so wrong?

"Why don't you put the kettle on and make yourselves a cup of tea while we wait?" Raissa said. "There are some chocolate digestives in the cupboard. I do love a chocolate biscuit."

As Hope filled the kettle, she caught Allegra's eye and they both smiled.

In the distance came the wail of an ambulance. Raissa looked panicked. "What am I going to do with Nurey if they want me to stay at the hospital?"

"Do you know anyone locally who could look after him?" Jazz asked.

"What about your next-door neighbour?" Hope suggested.

"They're away in Dorset, visiting their daughter," Raissa replied.

"It's OK." Portia patted the dog on the head. "I can take him home with me tonight. My house is only round the corner. Do you have a mobile phone?"

"Yes, it should be on the table."

Hope went over to the table. The phone was perched on top of a pile of magazines. It was a really basic model, with no internet access. "Here you go," she said, handing it to Raissa.

"Thank you, dear."

"I'll give you my number," Portia said, "just in case you do have to stay at the hospital. If you give me yours I can call you and let you know how Nurey's doing. Don't worry, I'm a dog lover."

"I can vouch for that." Jazz grinned.

"And I have my own dog-walking service," Portia continued.

"I can vouch for that too," Jazz said.

Raissa gave a sigh of relief. "How on earth did you girls find me? You're like a band of guardian angels."

"Or Moonlight Dreamers," Hope said under her breath.

Allegra grinned.

Chapter Twenty-Five

As the girls watched the ambulance drive off, Jazz laughed and shook her head. "What a night!"

"It's not over yet," Portia said, bending down to pet Nurey. "Somehow I've got to explain to my parents how I popped out to see some friends and ended up coming home with this little guy."

"I bet you didn't think your dream of saving a dog would come true so quickly," Hope said.

"Or in such a random way," Allegra added.

"I'm just so glad he wasn't being mistreated," Portia said. "I hope Raissa's going to be OK. I don't want her evil stepson getting his hands on Nurey, or her house."

"Me too," Jazz agreed.

"I think she might have been a ballet dancer when she was younger," Allegra said. "There's an old photo of a ballet dancer on her bedroom wall."

"Yeah, it looked just like a younger version of her," Hope added.

"And I'm guessing her dog might be named after a famous ballet dancer called Nureyev," Allegra continued.

"I remember seeing a YouTube video about him," Hope said. "He was Russian, right?"

"Yeah. He was awesome." Allegra smiled.

Portia was so glad to see Allegra and Hope actually getting on. This really had been a night of miracles.

"I don't know about you but I'm starving," said Jazz. "Does anyone fancy having some chips down on the beach?"

"Absolutely." Hope took her phone from her pocket. "I'll just let my mum and dad know. My mum gets super stressed if I'm a minute late."

"Yeah, I'll message mine too," Jazz said.

Portia took her phone from her bag. She'd texted her mum and dad that she'd just heard from a former dog-walking client who was having some kind of emergency; sow the seed for the story she'd tell them when she arrived home with Nurey. As she was about to start typing, she noticed that Allegra was the only one not texting. Her parents were probably the cool kind who didn't mind what time she came home because they treated her like an adult. She pictured a beautiful, goddess-like mum, reclining on a couch. *Go out and have adventures, my free-spirited daughter*, she imagined her saying to Allegra. *You only live once, so enjoy it, and never be a slave to parental curfews.* Allegra didn't look like she was enjoying anything much, though; the downcast expression she'd been wearing earlier had returned as she scuffed the toe of her boot against the kerb.

* * *

"So, Portia has achieved her dream from last week," Jazz said, once they were all sitting on the beach, holding warm paper bags of salty chips. "And I'm happy to report that I went on my paddleboard twice and I actually enjoyed it – especially when you came on it too," she added, grinning at Hope.

"You went paddleboarding?" Allegra stared at Hope.

"Yes," Hope said, nodding. "Well, I sat on the board. Jazz did the paddling. It really helped," she said, looking out at the water.

"Helped what?" Jazz asked. Hope had definitely seemed like a different person tonight, way more confident and positive.

"Helped me achieve my dream from last week's meeting."

"What was your dream?" Portia asked, feeding Nurey a chip. "Sorry, do you mind me asking?"

"Not at all." Hope smiled. "It was – it was to face my fear about dying." She looked at Jazz and giggled. "Falling off the paddleboard about a hundred times definitely helped me do that."

Jazz laughed, then looked at Allegra and Portia. "Don't worry, I didn't take her that deep."

"Have you ever got stuck in a way of thinking about something?" Hope asked quietly. "And like, you know it's bad for you, but you just can't snap out of it."

"Yeah," Jazz replied. "I guess I was like that when I first moved here. I couldn't stop feeling sorry for myself. You guys have definitely snapped me out of it, though, so thank you."

It felt good to admit to the others how she'd been before, as if a weight had been lifted.

"Same here," Hope agreed.

"Me too," Allegra said quietly.

"Really?" Portia stared at Allegra. "How? If you don't mind me asking?"

All eyes turned to Allegra. Jazz really hoped she would answer. Allegra always looked so composed – so together – it was hard to imagine her getting stuck in anything.

Allegra took a chip from her bag. "It's not so much a way of thinking that I'm stuck in, it's my whole life."

Whoa, still waters clearly run deep, Jazz thought to herself. "What do you mean?" she asked gently.

"I just feel like I've made some really bad decisions." Allegra put the chip back in the bag and looked down, her long hair falling forwards, covering her face. "And I wish I could go back and change them." Her voice quivered like she might be about to cry.

Jazz leaned across and placed a hand on her arm. She really didn't know what to say – but she knew a man who did. "I think you need to play What Would Oscar Say?" she said, fumbling in her bag for the book.

"Oh yes, you should," Hope agreed.

"What is it?" Allegra sniffed.

"Take this," Jazz said, passing her the book, "and think of the problem you're facing, then turn it into a question. Like, how can I change my life for the better? Or, how can I make up for the bad decisions I made? When you've got your question, say it in your head to the book."

"OK." Allegra looked down at the book. "Now what?"

"Open it on a random page and that's your answer from Oscar."

"The guy who wrote the starlight quote?"

"Yep."

"OK." Allegra flicked the book open.

"What does it say?" Hope asked.

Jazz held her breath. She really hoped the book's magic would work again.

"It says, '*When a man is old enough to do wrong he should be old enough to do right also*'," Allegra replied.

Jazz's heart sank. It didn't really sound like the kind of motivational quote Allegra needed, but to her surprise, Allegra started nodding her head.

"I love this!"

"You do?" Jazz couldn't hide her surprise.

"Yes. Can I take a photo of it?"

"Of course."

As Jazz watched Allegra take a photo of the page, she breathed a sigh of relief. The third Moonlight Dreamers meeting hadn't gone at all as planned, but if anything, it seemed all the better for it!

As Allegra climbed the last flight of stairs to her flat, she repeated the Oscar Wilde quote in her head. She'd been chanting it like a mantra all the way back from the beach. Ever since she'd had her run-in with Alf, she'd been wondering if maybe she'd been unfair, unleashing all of her anger upon him. After all, he had a pretty horrendous time at home with his dad. She certainly didn't want to add to that. And it wasn't as if he'd forced her to go out with him; she'd wanted it as well. She should have ended things in a more mature way. As that Oscar Wilde guy said, if you were old enough to do the wrong thing, you were old enough to take responsibility and do the right thing too. Allegra opened the door and saw that the hall light was on. She could have sworn she hadn't turned it on before she left. Her mum had drilled it into her enough times not to waste electricity.

"Allegra!" Magdalena came flying out of the kitchen, looking distraught. "Where have you been?"

"Out." Allegra's pulse quickened. What should she say? She was meant to be in bed with the flu. Magdalena was meant to be on a romantic date and staying out late – the pubs hadn't even shut yet.

"Where? With who?"

"Chantelle."

Magdalena frowned. "No, you haven't. I called her when you wouldn't answer your phone."

Crap! Allegra had put her phone on silent and hadn't looked at it since seeing Alf. "*What?* Why?"

"Because I was worried."

"Why?"

"What do you mean, why?" Magdalena came closer and Allegra saw that her eyes were red, as if she'd been crying. "You've been sick all week and then you suddenly disappear. You're my daughter."

"And you were out on a date."

"What's that supposed to mean?"

"Well, if you were that bothered about how I was feeling, you wouldn't have left me." Allegra knew it was a low blow but she had to do something to deflect her mum's anger.

A horrible silence fell.

"But I thought you'd be OK. I often go out in the evenings and leave you on your own."

"Exactly."

"You're fourteen."

"I know."

Another silence. Allegra could practically see Magdalena's mind spinning like a roulette wheel as she decided on which approach to take.

"I can't believe you're being like this. I've had a horrible evening and then I get home to find my daughter missing, and when you do reappear you're really mean to me."

Clearly the wheel had landed on playing the victim.

"I wasn't missing, I'd gone out."

"But not with your friends."

"Not with *those* friends."

"Then who were you with?"

"Some other friends, new friends."

Magdalena sighed. "And you didn't think to text me or leave me a note?"

"Oh for god's sake."

"Don't talk to me like that, Allegra. I am the mother here."

"Then act like one!" Allegra yelled, pushing past her and storming into her bedroom. *If you're old enough to do wrong you should be old enough to do right also!* She sat on her bed, her knees pulled up to her chin, watching the door and waiting for Magdalena to come storming in. But all remained quiet. Then she heard the soft click of Magdalena's bedroom door shutting. What a night! Allegra thought back to seeing Raissa lying there helpless on the kitchen floor, and how she'd thought of her abuela, living on her own in the Spanish mountains. Sofia was in her early seventies and sprightly for her age but she wouldn't be that way for ever. One day in the not-too-distant future she would be as old and frail as Raissa and yet Allegra had chosen not to see her this summer. Well, if Allegra was old enough to do wrong she should be old enough to put things right. She took out her phone, opened her email app and began to write...

Dear Abuela,

I'm so sorry if I hurt you by turning down your invitation to come and stay with you in the summer. You didn't reply to my other email so I guess you must be upset with me. I just want you to know that I'm truly sorry. I miss you so much, and not just your cooking!

I miss your words of wisdom. I could really do with them right now. Please forgive me. I understand if you don't want to invite me to stay again but I would love it if we could have a phone chat.

Your loving granddaughter,

Allegra

xxxx

As Allegra pressed SEND, there was a knock on the door. "Come in."

Magdalena walked in, her cheeks shiny from tears and streaked with mascara.

Allegra felt a knot of worry tighten inside her. "Mum, what's happened?"

"I'm so sorry," Magdalena said, perching on the end of the bed. "I thought – I thought you liked the freedom I give you."

"I do – I just…" Allegra broke off, unsure what to say. The truth was, she did like it, just not all the time.

"When I was your age, your abuela was so strict – always wanting to know where I was and who I was with, always demanding I was home before sunset – it drove me crazy."

"I know, it's just that sometimes I wish…"

"What?"

"That you could be a bit more like that with me. Like, not too much, but just more like a parent. Sometimes it feels like I'm living with another teenager."

Magdalena sighed. "I need to have a life too, though, outside of the salon and you."

"I know. I get that. I do."

"You just need me to be there for you more as well?"

"Yes."

"OK." Magdalena opened her arms. "Hug?"

Allegra leaned into her embrace.

"I hate falling out with you," Magdalena murmured into her hair.

"Me too." The tension in Allegra began to ease.

"And I've had such a rubbish night," Magdalena continued. Allegra felt her start to quiver. "Jonny didn't show up or reply to any of my messages. I think he's ghosted me."

"Don't worry, Mum, it's his loss."

As Allegra stroked her mum's hair, she couldn't help groaning inside. So much for Magdalena being the parent. Still, she couldn't expect things to change overnight, and at least she'd told her how she felt.

Chapter Twenty-Six

Dear Moonlight Dreamers,

Happy Friday! I've just heard from Raissa and they're keeping her in hospital for her hip op. The good news is, my parents have said that I can look after Nurey until she's back on her feet. Maybe they aren't out to thwart all of my dreams after all! He's so cute the whole family instantly fell in love with him – even my brother Darius, who right now seems to hate everything! Anyway, I told Raissa I'd come and visit her tomorrow and I wondered if you'd like to come with me? It could be the first official Moonlight Dreamers outing! ☺

Let me know what you think.

Portia x

Hope had wanted to get to the girls' changing rooms before the rest of her class arrived but unfortunately her form tutor made her stay behind after registration. By the time she got to the changing room it was full. As usual, Chantelle was holding court, talking loudly to her gaggle of fawning followers about how she was planning to get her belly button pierced.

"What are you doing here?" she asked as soon as she saw Hope, her over-plucked eyebrows creasing into a scowl.

"Don't worry, I'm not staying," Hope replied, scanning the room for Ms Sykes.

"Why not?" said a voice from behind her. Allegra's voice.

"Leggy!" Chantelle exclaimed. "Where the hell have you been? Why aren't you answering my texts? Your mum called me last night asking where you were."

"I know," Allegra replied, then asked Hope again, "Why won't you be staying?"

"Because..." Hope broke off. She really didn't want to give Chantelle the satisfaction of hearing her say it out loud.

"Because of her heart, innit?" Chantelle snapped.

"But you're allowed to do some exercise, right?" Allegra asked Hope.

"Yeah."

"Then you should stay." Allegra turned to Chantelle. "She should stay," she said firmly.

"Leggy, what the hell?" Chantelle's scowl deepened. "Why are you standing up for her?"

"Why are you picking on her?" Allegra returned her scowl.

An ominous silence fell as the rest of the class glanced nervously between Chantelle and Allegra. This had never happened before – a battle of the queen bees – and it was impossible to tell who would win. Hope felt nervous for

Allegra. She might be super popular but she didn't have Chantelle's edge, or her physical strength.

Chantelle stood up. "I'm not picking on her. I'm trying to protect the rest of us."

"Oh please!" Allegra gave a sarcastic laugh. "Since when have you ever protected anyone? You're just a bully."

Hope's pulse quickened. Much as she appreciated Allegra's sudden show of support, she couldn't help feeling that it was going to backfire. Thankfully, just at that moment, Ms Sykes bounded into the room, clad in her tracksuit and holding her whistle.

"Wow, you lot are very quiet — what's happened?"

No one replied.

"Is everything OK?" she asked, her smile fading.

"Yes, Miss," Allegra muttered, going over to the nearest bench and hanging her coat on a peg.

"Good." Ms Sykes turned to Hope. "We're going to be doing some gym work today, Hope. You can take it at your own pace, if you feel up to it?"

As all eyes turned to Hope, she realized that this was one of those rare pivotal moments. How she responded to Ms Sykes' question would affect her life for some time to come, and Allegra's. She swallowed hard before replying. "I'm up to it, thank you."

All through gym, Allegra felt Chantelle's eyes boring into her. Even when she had her back to her. *You're old enough to do the right thing*, she reminded herself. And she *had* done the right thing sticking up for Hope, she was sure of it. As soon as she'd called Chantelle out, the weight of her guilt had lifted. And in spite of the nervousness now bubbling away in her stomach, she still felt a sense of defiance. She was sick of Chantelle picking on other people. It had always made her uncomfortable but she'd turned a blind eye before. Not any more. Although Allegra still wasn't sure who she was or what she wanted in life, she knew without a shadow of a doubt that she didn't want to be that person.

Back in the changing room after class the chatter was muted, as if everyone was waiting for the storm brewing between Allegra and Chantelle to break. The next lesson was Maths and they were in different sets, so it would be morning break or lunchtime when things would come to a head. For once, Chantelle got changed in record speed. As she walked past Allegra, she hissed, "I'll see you later." She might have said it quietly but from her icy tone it was definitely a threat.

Allegra concentrated on putting her shoes on. Hope came and sat beside her.

"Thank you," she said quietly.

"No need to thank me," Allegra replied. "I was just trying to do the right thing."

Hope nodded. Allegra wanted to reach out to her, say something about last night, but she felt too ashamed. She should have stuck up for Hope long ago, back when Alf picked on her outside the café.

"See you later then?" Hope said, as if she was asking a question.

"Yeah, see you."

At first break, Allegra slipped into the disabled toilet down by the school reception. She didn't have the stomach to face Chantelle just yet, especially as she now had to deal with the double whammy of having annoyed both her and Alf. She pictured them comparing notes about her, whinging about what a bitch she was, and tears began to burn in her eyes. *Moonlight Dreamers are proud of being different*, she reminded herself. Looking for a distraction, she took her phone from her blazer pocket and saw that she had some new emails. One from Portia and one from – her heart began to sing – her abuela! As she clicked it open, her stomach churned. If Sofia was writing to tell her how angry she was, it would be the final straw.

My darling granddaughter,

I should be the one apologizing to you! I'm so sorry, I hadn't seen your previous email. I've been avoiding the World Wide Interweb, to be honest with you, as I'm being pursued by a suitor from the next village and I'm trying to spurn his advances. It's a very long story! I shall fill you in when we next speak. And of course I would love to have a phone chat with you, whenever you like. I wasn't angry that you didn't come this summer. It might have been a long

*time ago but I can still remember what it's like to be a teenager
and I guessed that hanging around with an old lady might not be
as much fun as spending the summer with your friends. You are
always welcome here, my darling, so just let me know whenever
you'd like to come and I shall book you a ticket. Looking forward
to speaking with you.*

All my love,

Abuela
xxxxxxx

Allegra wanted to dance with joy! Sofia wasn't angry with
her – she still wanted to see her! The prism of her life widened,
no longer limited to Chantelle and Alf, no longer confined to
school and the park. Now it contained mountains and olive
groves and friends who sat by the sea conjuring their dreams
by moonlight and searching for the stars. She took a moment
to compose herself then clicked on Portia's message. As
she read it, her relief grew. Raissa was OK. Portia had been
allowed to take care of her dog. *And* Allegra had an invite to
go out with the Moonlight Dreamers tomorrow. She replied
to Portia, telling her she'd love to come to the hospital, then
she replied to Sofia, asking if they could have a phone chat
that evening. She looked in the mirror and sighed. "It's going
to be OK," she whispered to her reflection.

* * *

Jazz sat down at one of the computers in the school library and stared at the Google search bar. What should she look up today to try and fill her lunchbreak? *What should you do if you hate your school?* she typed and pressed enter. The top result that came up was from a site called Surviving School. *If you hate school*, it said, *the most obvious solution is to leave school.*

Leave school. The words buzzed in Jazz's head. She looked around the library. The other students were either hunched over their books or absorbed in their screens. No one here would even notice if she disappeared. No one here would care. It was a horrible feeling. She looked at her phone, at her last WhatsApp message from Lisa. **That's so cool. I'm so happy for you!** she'd written in response to Jazz's message. Jazz couldn't be bothered to tell her the truth about how things were going at school – it was too tragic. So she'd said it was "awesome" and she'd made a "ton of friends". That last part wasn't a complete lie, she tried to console herself. She had made some friends, just not at Cedars.

The most obvious solution ... is to leave school. Jazz shut down the computer. She stood up and put on her jacket. She walked out of the library. She walked down the corridor. The students she passed looked straight through her. It was as if she'd developed the power of invisibility, which she'd always thought would be a really cool super power. She didn't think that way any more. It turned out that invisibility was terrible for a person's mental health. *Leave school.* She walked out of the nearest fire exit, down the path and out of the main gates.

She'd left school.

The bus ride home passed in a daze. Jazz knew that walking out of school was bound to end badly, that it was only a sticking plaster not a solution, but at least she was free – for now. When she reached home, she cautiously opened the front door, listening for any sound of her parents. She knew Mikey was out at a local studio and Cheryl was at work but it would be just her luck if one of them had come home early for some reason. Thankfully, the house was empty.

She went into her bedroom and looked out at the ocean. The water was a murky grey and the waves were so frothy she longed for her surfboard. She'd learned from her online research that there were other parts of Britain where you could surf. A place called Cornwall seemed to be the favourite, but it was miles away, to the west of the country. Maybe she shouldn't just leave school. Maybe she should leave Brighton too. Pack up a bag and her board and get on a train to Cornwall.

But what about Mum and Dad? a goody-goody voice said in her head. *What about them?* she responded sullenly. *They didn't think about me when they upped and moved us all the way around the globe.* Another retort: *But what about the Moonlight Dreamers?* She thought of Portia, Hope and Allegra and her mind flashed back to Raissa's kitchen. What was it Raissa had called them? A band of guardian angels. To Raissa they'd looked like a proper group of friends, even though they'd only known each other a couple of weeks. Surely that had to mean something? Jazz felt so confused there was only one thing for it – only one place she could hope to find focus and peace.

Once she'd changed into her wetsuit she fetched her paddleboard from the cupboard and made her way down to the water. It was a lot livelier than it had looked from upstairs, the waves hungrily licking the stones. It was hardly the perfect climate for paddleboarding. But that might make it a bit more exciting, she reasoned, a bit more like surfing. She strode into the water, gasping as a wave crashed in over her face. She positioned the board beside her, waited for a gap between waves and clambered on. She remained kneeling for a second, making sure she was at the sweet spot and able to keep her balance. Another wave rolled in, lifting the board and sending her flying. She needed to get out further, deeper.

She swam for a bit, pushing the board in front of her. With every wave that splashed into her face she felt her confusion and sorrow being washed away.

"I am the sea and the sea is me," she said with a giggle, remembering the line her surf instructor had told her as a kid. "All right, calm down sea," she called as another huge wave lifted her high. She wriggled back into position and up onto the board. "OK, let's do this," she muttered. A wave was building in the distance so Jazz got into a standing position, holding her paddle aloft. "I am the sea and the sea is me!" she called louder, like a crazy person. Maybe she was crazy. Maybe she had finally flipped. Whatever. It was good. She felt fully alive again. The wave grew and grew and then it was beneath her, lifting the board, and a rush of energy shot through her. And for a glorious moment, she wasn't trying to paddleboard in freezing-cold Britain, she was back home, riding the surf in the sun. Somehow she managed to stay on the board as the wave crashed beneath her. The water pulled her out further, deeper. She wiped the ocean spray from her eyes, tasting the salt on her lips, and, looking back to the shore, she saw that the house had suddenly grown a lot smaller.

"Crap!" She attempted to paddle back inland but the current was too powerful.

Maybe it would be easier to swim. Jazz slipped from the board as another wave came thundering in. It tossed her high and when she came crashing down again, the paddle slid from her grasp. She looked around frantically. It was already several metres away, further from the shore. *It's OK*, she told herself. *You're used to this.* She started swimming towards the shore, pushing the board in front of her but for every metre she gained, the current sucked her back two.

In the distance she saw a figure come out onto the deck of the house next door. *Focus*, she told herself and she tried to swim again, but the board was too big and cumbersome and the waves were too powerful. What if she was stuck here for ever, trying to swim forwards but being sucked backwards, like in one of those horrible dreams where you're running up a hill but never get to the top? What if she drowned?

Jazz gasped as a wave hit her full on and her mouth filled with salt water.

I don't want to drown. All of her thoughts suddenly focused into those five small words. *I... Don't... Want... To... Drown.* Even though her school was crap and her classmates were stuck-up. Even though she wasn't able to surf. Even though she desperately missed her friends from home. Even though... She still didn't want to drown. She wanted to see the Moonlight Dreamers again. She thought of Portia, Hope and Allegra standing on the shore, willing her back in and she pushed the board away and began to swim and swim. *I don't want to drown. I want to live*, she thought with every stroke. *I want to live. I want to live. I want to live.*

Chapter Twenty-Seven

As Hope stood in the queue in the school canteen, she saw Allegra glide in like a swan, neck straight, head aloft. She was so graceful. Even when she'd been arguing with Chantelle earlier, she'd somehow managed to stay cool. If only Hope could be more like that, instead of getting so flustered about everything. She glanced over to the table where Allegra and her friends always sat, at the back of the room. Chantelle was already there, hunched in conversation with some of their other friends. Allegra walked straight past them, over to the drinks machine. She put some coins in the slot and took out a bottle of juice. Then she walked straight past the table again, head up, focusing firmly on the door. Everyone watched. Chantelle said something and there were a few sniggers as Allegra made it to the door and back outside.

Feeling a sudden compulsion to follow her, Hope quickly paid for her lunch and hurried out, just in time to see Allegra disappear round the corner in the direction of the bike racks. Hope followed and found her sitting on a bench, sipping her drink.

"Hey," she said.

"Hey," Allegra replied.

"I just wanted to check that you were OK."

"Really?" Allegra's eyes widened, like she didn't quite believe her.

"Yeah. After the drama in PE."

"I should have stood up for you ages ago," Allegra said quietly. "I'm sorry."

"It's OK. Do you mind...? Can I join you?"

"Of course." Allegra shifted along the bench.

"Sandwich?" Hope asked, opening the pack and holding it out.

"Sure." Allegra took one of the sandwiches. "Thank you."

They sat and ate in silence for a while, but it was the kind of silence that didn't feel awkward. The kind of silence shared by friends.

Jazz kicked out and felt something beneath her foot. Something solid. Something very much like the ground. She looked up and saw the shore in front of her and her house back to its normal size. Shirley from next door had come down onto the beach with Reggie and was waving at her. She was with someone. Oh no! It was her dad. What was he doing home so early? Jazz stood up, her legs buckling slightly.

"Sweetheart, are you all right?" Mikey called over the crash of the waves. Reggie began barking beside him.

Jazz nodded, trying to catch her breath. "My board isn't, though." She turned back towards the ocean and glimpsed a flash of colour as her board drifted closer to the horizon.

"Looks as if it's heading for France," Shirley said. "I thought you were too at one point. That's why I went and got your father."

As relief flooded her body, Jazz felt the sudden inappropriate urge to laugh. She'd made it back to land. Admittedly she was probably about to get in a whole heap of trouble for skiving off school but at least she hadn't drowned. She bent over to try and catch her breath.

"I was just about to call the coastguard," Shirley continued. "What were you thinking, taking your board out in those conditions?"

"It's all right, Shirley. I'll take it from here," Mikey said. He came over to Jazz and put his arm round her shoulders. As Shirley made her way across the beach to her house, Jazz began shivering uncontrollably.

Mikey hugged her tighter. "Bloody hell, darlin', were you trying to give your old dad a heart attack? I was about to strip off and dive in there after you."

"I'm sorry. I didn't realize the water was so rough."

They went up onto the deck and into the kitchen. Mikey headed straight for the kettle. "I think you need a strong cup of tea. I think we both do." He fetched her a towel and wrapped it round her. "What are you doing home from school so early?"

"I left early."

"Why?"

"Because I couldn't stand it any more," she said quickly before she could chicken out.

"What?" He stared at her.

"They all hate me and no one talks to me and I can't stand it."

"Bloody hell!" Mikey leaned against the counter and scratched his head. "I thought you'd made friends. Those girls who came round…"

"I told you, they're not from school. No one at school talks to me."

"But why? How could no one like you?" He looked so shocked it made her want to hug him and cry in equal measure.

"Well, I might have made a dig about the days of Britain ruling the world being over – in front of the whole class – but that was only because they kept blanking me."

Mikey started to grin. "Oh dear."

"Exactly. I've got nothing in common with them, Dad. They're all so stuck-up."

Mikey began pacing up and down, the way he always did when he was trying to figure out some kind of musical issue for work. Jazz held her breath, preparing herself for the inevitable lecture that was bound to follow.

"There's really no one there that you get along with?"

Hearing it said out loud like this made her feel even worse. She hugged the towel around her and bit her lip to try and stop herself crying. "It's not me, OK? I never had problems making friends back at home. And I've made friends with some other girls over here. I just – I don't fit in there."

Mikey looked really upset. "Oh, darlin', your mum and I only sent you there because we wanted you to have a good education. We thought it would be fun for you to go to a British private school. We thought it would – you know – make up for you having to come so far from home."

"I know, Dad, and I appreciate it but I don't think I'm cut out for a school like that."

He nodded. "So, the friends you have made, the ones who were round here, what school do they go to?"

"The local state schools."

"And they're happy there?"

"Yeah. I guess. I mean, they never moan about it the way I do."

"All right, let me have a word with your mum when she gets home."

"Are you serious?" Jazz was so excited her voice came out in a squeak.

"Of course. We want you to be happy, darlin'. Obviously I don't know what the procedure would be for you to change schools, or if they have any places available at the local state schools, but if your mum agrees, we'll look into it, OK?"

"OK." Jazz flung her arms around him. "Thank you."

"No problem. But promise me one thing."

"What?"

"No more extreme paddleboarding!"

Jazz laughed. "Don't worry. I promise!"

Chapter Twenty-Eight

"We're here to see Raissa," Portia announced as the Moonlight Dreamers gathered around the reception desk at the hospital.

"Goodness me, she's popular," the nurse chuckled, looking at them. "You'll find her in the third bed on the left, by the window."

"Thank you." Portia led the other girls into the ward. Even though it was slightly bizarre to be in a hospital on a Saturday afternoon, visiting an old lady she'd only met once – and under the weirdest of circumstances – she knew there was nothing she'd rather be doing. She only hoped Raissa was all right; she'd looked so frail when they'd last seen her.

"Girls!" A cry rang out from the bed by the window. Raissa was propped up against a bank of pillows, her white hair pulled up into a bun and a beaming smile on her face. She was holding a pen and there was a folded newspaper on her lap. A shaft of pale sunlight was shining in through the blinds, making her face glow.

"Hi, Raissa," Jazz said. "Wow, you look so much better!"

Allegra and Hope murmured in agreement.

"My guardian angels," Raissa said, as they gathered around her bed. "I'm so happy to see you."

"It's great to see you too," Portia exclaimed. "Nurey says hello. I took some photos of him for you." She sat on a chair by the head of the bed and took out her phone.

"How are you feeling?" Hope asked.

"A lot better," Raissa replied. "Or at least I will be as soon as I've had my op on Monday. Sit down, please." She gestured at the other chairs by the bed. "I don't think I'll ever be able to thank you enough for what you've done."

"It was nothing," Jazz replied breezily.

"No, it wasn't," Raissa said with a firm shake of her head. "I dread to think what might have happened if you girls hadn't showed up."

"Yes, well, we did, so that's all that matters," Portia replied.

"It wasn't just you helping me from the fall, though," Raissa continued. "You've given me a – how do you say it? – a wake-up call."

"What do you mean?" Allegra asked.

Raissa sighed. "I'm ashamed to say that in recent years I've let fear get the better of me."

"What were you afraid of?" Hope asked.

"What *wasn't* I afraid of?" Raissa gave a sad laugh. "I was afraid of getting older. Afraid of having a hip replacement and losing Nurey. Afraid of being all alone."

"Fear is the worst," Hope said softly.

"Yes, yes, it is," Raissa agreed. "I felt so lost after my beloved husband died. He was everything to me."

"Had you been together a long time?" Allegra asked.

"Not long enough." Raissa gazed dreamily out of the window. "We met when I'd just turned forty. We'd both been married before but to the wrong people."

"What do you mean, the wrong people?" Allegra asked, looking really interested.

"They weren't our true soulmates."

"How do you know if someone's your true soulmate?" Allegra blurted out. "Sorry, I don't mean to be nosy."

"That's all right, dear." Raissa's smile grew. "You know because the moment you first meet them you don't want to say, 'hello', you want to say, 'hello *again*'."

Portia stared at Raissa blankly. What did she mean? And why was Allegra so keen to talk about soulmates? She wanted to chat with Raissa about Nurey.

"Hello *again*," Allegra echoed. "So it feels as if you already know them?"

"That's right." Raissa smiled and, for a moment, Portia saw a beautiful young woman beneath the white hair and the wrinkles. "The moment I laid eyes on Jacques I felt as if I'd known him for ever. We instantly became inseparable. I guess we wanted to make up for lost time. And meeting in our forties, we knew that we didn't have all the time in the world. Although in the end I was lucky enough to have thirty-five years with him."

Portia quickly did the maths. If Raissa had met Jacques when she was forty and he'd died three years ago, that made her around seventy-eight.

"I'd got so used to having him as my constant companion," Raissa continued, "I'd forgotten that for the forty years before we met I'd managed just fine!" She laughed. "My younger self would be horrified at the frightened mouse I've become."

"Don't say that," Allegra said. "You're still the same person. You just forgot her for a while, that's all."

"My, aren't you a wise one?" Raissa looked at her and smiled. "I think you're all wonderful. You remind me of the friends I had back in Moscow when I was your age."

"You're from Russia?" Allegra asked, eyes widening.

"Yes, although that feels like another lifetime ago." She chuckled. "My girlfriends and I had such adventures. I bet you do too."

"We certainly hope to," Jazz said.

"So lovely," Raissa murmured. "You must treasure this time together, treasure your friendships."

"I do," Allegra said quietly and Portia noticed her and Hope exchanging shy smiles. Jazz had clearly noticed too from the way she was beaming in their direction. And then Portia couldn't help grinning too. It was so strange. If someone had told her before that she'd be able to make one good girl friend, she'd have been wary, but to have made three – that was really something.

The girls ended up staying with Raissa for over an hour while she regaled them with tales of her childhood in Russia and touring the world as a ballet dancer. As she talked, her eyes sparkled and her whole body became animated. *We helped make this happen*, Portia realized and it filled her with joy. Raissa might think of the Moonlight Dreamers as her guardian angels but Portia preferred to think of them as graphic novel heroes. She might have got it wrong about Nurey being mistreated, but they'd still managed to save the day by rescuing Raissa – and in more ways than one, by the sound of it. And she got to take care of Nurey until Raissa was better too. Yes, if her life were a graphic novel, this image of the girls sitting around a giggling Raissa with the sun streaming in on them would be the final happy frame in the story.

Chapter Twenty-Nine

As Allegra made her way through the estate, she glanced left and right for any sign of Chantelle and the rest of the gang. The sky was darkening and the street lamps had come on, casting the pavement in pools of amber light. After her conversation with Raissa she felt more certain than ever that she'd done the right thing by standing up to Chantelle. It had been so reassuring to hear the older woman talk about losing sight of who she really was. And the way she'd explained about how you know when you've met your soulmate confirmed to Allegra that she and Alf should definitely not be together. She turned onto the road leading down to the sea. When they'd left the hospital Jazz had asked them what they were doing later. As none of them had plans, she'd invited them to the beach for an impromptu Moonlight Dreamers meeting. Now that Allegra had finally fixed things with Hope she felt excited at the prospect of sitting with the others on the beach and talking about their dreams, especially as she had made a breakthrough in one of hers.

The girls had arranged to meet by the old pier. A bracing wind coming in off the sea had swept the beach clean of people so it was easy to spot the other Moonlight Dreamers sitting by the water's edge. The silvery moon hung in the sky above the skeletal remains of the pier, making it look spookier and more atmospheric than ever.

"Hello!" Allegra called cheerily as she made her way across the pebbles.

The others greeted her warmly, especially Hope, she noted with a grin.

"I've got something for you," Hope said shyly, as Allegra came and sat beside her. She handed her a postcard. On one side she'd written something in gold and on the other there was a picture of some mountains. "The quote is the one I got when I played What Would Oscar Say? – I thought you might find it inspiring. And the mountains are actually in France but I thought they could symbolize the mountains where your grandma lives, to help you visualize your dream coming true."

Allegra was so touched by Hope's gift she didn't know what to say at first. "Wow – thank you. That's so thoughtful of you. I actually have good news on that front," she said.

"You do?" Jazz looked at her eagerly.

"Yes." Allegra heard the crunch of footsteps on the stones behind her, probably a dog walker. "I spoke to my abuela last night and…" She noticed Portia staring at something over her shoulder. Or was it some*one*?

"All right, Leggy?"

Allegra's body seemed to turn to stone at the sound of Alf's voice. Hope looked equally horrified.

"What's going on?" he said.

Finally Allegra regained the use of her body and she turned to face him. He was wearing a black tracksuit with a baseball cap pulled down low over his face. She looked back at the other girls, all staring at him. Her worst nightmare was coming true: her two worlds were about to collide.

"Do you know him?" Portia asked.

Alf gave a sarcastic laugh. "Of course she knows me." He looked down at Allegra. "So what's going on?"

Allegra scrambled to stand up, almost losing her footing on the stones in her rush.

"Are these your famous friends from dancing?"

"Definitely not." Portia grinned at Jazz and Hope. "According to my brother I look like a demented wind turbine when I dance."

Allegra winced.

Alf stared at Portia then frowned at Allegra. "What's going on?" he asked for the third time.

"How did you know I was here?" Allegra's shock began to fade, replaced by anger. "Did you follow me?"

"What am I supposed to do? You're not replying to any of my texts."

"I don't think we've got anything left to say to each other after the other day." She looked down at the other girls, all staring up at her. Even Portia's customary cheeriness had now faded.

"Why are you being so moody?" Alf asked.

Embarrassed, Allegra grabbed Alf's sleeve and started

pulling him away. "Come on, let's talk in private." She glanced back over her shoulder at the girls. "I'm really sorry. I'll be back in a minute."

They walked up to the top of the beach in silence. Music was pumping from one of the beachfront bars near by. It seemed jarring; way too jolly a soundtrack for what had just happened – what was *still* happening.

"Who are they then?" Alf asked, nodding back towards the group on the beach.

"Friends."

"But not from your old dance class?"

"No." This was excruciating. She dreaded to think how Hope would be feeling at Alf's surprise appearance.

"So how come you're blanking Chantelle?"

She glared at him. "Have you been having another of your little chats about me?"

"No, Robbo told me. He heard it off Michelle."

Great.

"I don't get why you're being so moody. Are you seeing someone else?"

"No!" she snapped. "Are you really that arrogant that you can't imagine I'd rather be single than be with you?"

She was expecting him to be angry but instead she saw hurt flicker in his eyes and he stepped back as if she'd slapped him.

"Wow," he said softly.

They stood for a moment, staring at the floor. Allegra was

the first to break the silence. "I'm sorry."

"I don't know what I did." He scuffed the toe of his snowy white trainer on the ground. "I'm not arrogant, Leggy. How can I be when my own dad tells me what a piece of shit I am every day? I just…" He broke off, looking as if he was on the verge of tears.

Allegra felt a pang of guilt. "You're not a piece of shit, OK? I just don't think we're right together."

He stared at her blankly. "But we look all right together, don't we?"

"Yeah, but it's not about how we look." She gazed at the sea, hoping for inspiration. An image of Raissa came into her mind. "When I first got to know you I didn't think, Hello *again*."

"What?" He was staring at her like she was crazy.

"I don't think you're my soulmate. And I don't think I'm yours."

"Soulmate?" He gave a sad little grin. "It's a bit early for that lovey-dovey stuff, isn't it?"

"No, I don't think it is. I think when you're right for each other you know instantly."

"Wow." He scratched his head. "This is all a bit heavy."

Allegra felt a spark of hope. "See, we're not suited. You need to be with someone more like you."

"What? A football fan?" He chuckled.

"Possibly." She smiled at him. Then the quote she'd got from that Oscar Wilde book popped into her head and she imagined a posh old Englishman saying, 'When a man is old enough to do wrong he should be old enough to do right also!'

"I'm sorry if I hurt you," she said quietly.

In the moment's silence that followed she hardly dared breathe. Would he accept her apology, or would he want to start another fight?

"I'm sorry too," he muttered. "I didn't mean those things I said, about you being boring and that, and a bitch. Although, to be fair, I still think you are a bit over the top with the whole soulmate thing." He looked at her and grinned.

"I can accept that," she said, grinning back at him, and the irony of the situation wasn't lost on her. In breaking up, she and Alf were having their deepest moment of connection.

"All right then," he said, adjusting his cap. "I suppose I'd better get going."

"OK. Take care, yeah?"

"Yeah, you too." He looked at her for a moment, then slapped her on the side of her arm like he was saying goodbye to one of his mates. And with that, he turned and sauntered off along the seafront. A peal of laughter rang out from the bar and again it was the most inappropriate soundtrack. As Allegra watched him go, she experienced a strange mixture of relief and sorrow. Getting together with Alf had been her dream for so long. But maybe that was the thing about dreams, she thought as she turned to go back to the girls, maybe you needed some of them to go wrong, to help you figure out what – or who – was right.

"OK, so that was a little unexpected," Jazz quipped as she, Hope and Portia watched Allegra trudging up the beach with their uninvited guest.

"He's her boyfriend," Hope said, looking miserable. "Or at least, he was."

"Yeah, it didn't sound like he was all that happy with her," Portia mused.

"He's an idiot," Hope snapped.

Jazz's heart sank. Allegra and Hope had been getting on so well. She glanced up at the promenade, where Allegra and the guy were standing, heads bowed, deep in conversation.

"My parents said I can look for a new school," she said, deciding to change the subject and hopefully lighten the mood.

"No way!" Portia exclaimed.

"Yep. Let's just say everything came to a head yesterday." Jazz gazed out at the calm sea, shimmering in the moonlight. It was hard to imagine that the very same sea had been tossing her around like a wild cat toying with a mouse just the day before. But that was why she loved the water so much. It was impossible to tame.

"Come to my school, please!" Portia implored. "It really isn't that bad as far as schools go and it definitely isn't as snobby as Cedars."

"Funnily enough, I was looking at your school's website earlier," Jazz replied. "It looks like you have a great sports department."

"Yeah, well, I wouldn't have used that as a selling point," Portia joked. "But if that's what it takes for you to come there, then so be it."

Jazz laughed.

"And it's only fair that you come to my school," Portia continued. "Seeing as Hope and Allegra are already schoolmates. If you went there too, I'd be all on my own – a Moonlight Dreamer out on a limb. A star-gazer cut adrift in a solitary gutter. A—"

"All right, all right," Jazz laughed, cutting in.

They all looked up at the sound of Allegra making her way back over the stones.

"Are you OK?" Jazz asked.

"Yes, I'm so sorry about that. He was my – we were going out for a while, but I broke up with him the other day." Allegra sat back down beside Hope.

"You did?" Hope asked.

"Yeah. We weren't right for each other." Allegra gave a sad smile. "Let's just say Raissa isn't the only one who lost sight of who she really is."

"I can relate to that too," Jazz said.

"And me." Hope smiled.

"Wow." Portia raised her eyebrows. "Looks like I'm the only one in this group who actually has her act together."

The others laughed.

"So, everything's OK?" Jazz asked Allegra again, needing to be sure.

"Yeah, it is now," Allegra replied. "In fact, it's more than OK."

Jazz felt happiness unfurling inside her.

"You know that thing Raissa said about soulmates," Allegra said quietly, looking down at the pebbles.

"Yeah," Hope replied.

"Well, do you think it could be true about friends too?"

"How do you mean?" Jazz asked.

"Like, do you think you can get that 'hello *again*' feeling when you meet certain friends?" Allegra paused for a moment before continuing. "Because I think I feel like that with all of you."

"I feel like that too," Portia said.

"Same here." Hope smiled.

"Me too," Jazz said softly, and she felt her eyes begin to well up, but for once they were happy tears. She glanced up at the darkening sky and whispered a silent "thank you". Somehow, by some miracle, she had travelled right across the globe and found herself a new home with new friends. She'd looked up from the gutter and found three shining stars.

Chapter Thirty

Hey Amber,

How's it going? I'm sorry it's been a while since I last wrote. So much has been happening, and I'm very happy to report that it's all good! I've just started at a new school, where – guess what! – I already have a friend!!! One of my fellow Moonlight Dreamers, Portia, is a student there. She's the one I told you about who's obsessed with dogs and graphic novels. I'm so happy! Everything's going great with the other Moonlight Dreamers too. I don't know if it's all the sitting around talking about our dreams but I feel like I've known them for ever and now I can't imagine my life without them.

How's it going with the friend you made that day in the café? And the girl you met at the museum? I hope it's all good. We have a half-term holiday coming up and Mikey and Cheryl have promised to take me to Newquay in Cornwall so I can go surfing. I seriously cannot wait!!! Let me know your news!

Love, Jazz xx

* * *

Dear Jazz,

It was so lovely to get your message – and to hear you sounding so happy! It really fills me with joy to think of the magic of the Moonlight Dreamers bringing together another group of friends.

I'm glad to report that all is great here too. Yes, I'm still friends with Loren – we've actually decided to write a play together! I'm not sure if anything will come of it but it's a very fun creative process. I had to drop the girl I met at the museum as she turned out to be a bit of a blatherskite (a person who talks at great length without making much sense, which handily was my word of the day today ☺).

I hope you're able to visit me in Paris sometime – I'd love to show you the sights. Maybe you could bring the other Moonlight Dreamers – I brought Maali, Sky and Rose here a few years ago and we had the best time. Right, I'd better go as I'm meeting Loren for a cheese-and-wine-fuelled creative brainstorm down by the river. I've eaten so much cheese since I got here that if you cut me, I'd probably bleed milk!

Speak soon, dear cousin, and enjoy your weekend!

Amber

xx

* * *

As Hope woke up, she had the weirdest sensation that she was still dreaming. All she could see was bright turquoise. She blinked hard but the turquoise was still there, all around her. And then it came back to her — she'd stayed the night at Allegra's. She rolled over and looked down at Allegra still asleep on an inflatable mattress on the floor, her long brown hair splaying out on the pillow. If someone had told Hope a few weeks ago that Allegra was one day going to invite her for a sleepover — and that Hope was going to accept — she would have thought that they were crazy, but here they were. She lay on her back and gazed up at the constellation of glow-in-the-dark stars on the ceiling. It made Hope think of the quote on Jazz's postcard about everyone being in the gutter but some people looking at the stars. She cringed as she remembered her initial response to it. Now she'd got to know Allegra she realized that the quote had been right after all — life was difficult for everyone, no matter how beautiful or together a person might seem. But people always had the choice to focus on the positive.

She picked up her phone and saw a text from her mum: **Morning, love. Hope you slept well? xxx** Hope grinned. It had taken a lot for her mum to agree to her coming to this sleepover. It was the first time Hope had stayed away overnight since her diagnosis. And now, hopefully, she'd be allowed to visit Megan at half-term. Hope had been overjoyed when Meg had called to invite her. It turned out her sister hadn't totally forgotten about her after all. She gave a contented sigh. Life was different now that she had HCM but it didn't mean it had to be worse. In many ways, thanks to the Moonlight Dreamers, it was actually better.

"Hey," Allegra said sleepily from her bed on the floor.

"Morning." Hope sat up and took a glass of water and her pack of beta blockers from the nightstand, popping one from the strip of pills.

"Did you sleep OK?" Allegra asked, shifting herself upright.

"Yeah, great." Hope put the tablet in her mouth and swallowed it down with a gulp of water.

"I'll go and get us some tea and toast." Allegra got up and put on a brightly coloured satin kimono. "I can't wait to see Raissa today."

"Me too," Hope agreed, finishing the glass of water.

It was only when Allegra had gone to the kitchen that she realized she'd forgotten to count while taking her tablet. She lay back on the bed and grinned.

Portia giggled as Nurey strained on the lead. "All right, all right, I know you're dying to get home," she said. As they approached the front of Raissa's house, Portia paused. It was almost unrecognizable. The grass was freshly mown, the weeds were gone and two brightly painted ceramic pots bursting with geraniums and giant daisies stood either side of the front door. Portia had come up with the idea of giving Raissa's house and gardens a makeover while she was still in hospital recovering from her hip replacement and the other Moonlight Dreamers had readily agreed. To Portia's shock and slight embarrassment, Raissa's stepson, Roger, had helped too, arranging for the outside of the house to have a fresh coat of paint. Raissa had joked that he was only protecting his inheritance but Portia had to admit that he wasn't nearly as bad as she'd first imagined. He was a bit gruff and grumpy, yes, but definitely not a crazed animal abuser. One important lesson she'd learned recently was that you shouldn't rush to judge – whether it was about grumpy men or teenage girls.

Nurey pulled her up the garden path, yelping excitedly, and she opened the front door with Raissa's spare key. The house smelled of a delicious mixture of fresh baking and a rose-scented candle Allegra had bought.

"It's only me," Portia called. She let Nurey off the lead and he scampered down the hall into the kitchen.

"Hello, darling!" Raissa cried.

She followed Nurey to find Jazz sitting at the kitchen table looking at something on her phone and Raissa standing by the oven beside her walking frame. She was wearing a pair of smart black trousers and a pink polo neck. It had been four weeks since her operation and every time Portia saw her she looked younger and fitter.

"Hey, Portia," Jazz said with a grin. "I've just been showing Raissa where I'm going surfing in Cornwall."

"Cool," Portia replied, although if she was honest, she really couldn't see what there was to get so excited about — especially at this time of year. The sea would be freezing!

"You must have a Cornish cream tea while you're there." Raissa smiled. "The scones are so delicious and the cream is like nothing you've ever tasted. And talking of cakes, I've made us all some Russian teacakes," she said proudly, pointing to a plate of small round cakes on the table.

"They smell amazing," Portia replied. "How's your hip?"

"Oh, it's wonderful, my dear." Raissa's smile grew. "For the first time in two years I'm free from pain."

Just then the doorbell rang. "I'll get it," Portia offered.

She opened the front door to find Hope and Allegra chatting away. Allegra was in one of her really cool outfits again, teaming a grey-and-black vintage Minnie Mouse top with flared jeans and dusky pink high-top trainers. Hope looked great too, rosy-faced and smiling.

"How was your night?" Portia asked, barely able to believe that such former arch-enemies would have been able to spend the night under one roof without killing one another.

"Great!" Hope beamed.

"Yes, really fun. Mmm, something smells delicious," Allegra said as they came into the hallway.

"Raissa's been baking," Portia informed them.

"Happy days!" Allegra exclaimed and Hope giggled. As Portia followed them down the hallway to the kitchen, she found herself heartily agreeing — happy days indeed.

As soon as Allegra saw Raissa standing by a plate of freshly baked cakes, she felt compelled to run over and hug her. She looked so like her abuela. "You look great!" she exclaimed.

"Well, what a lovely greeting!" Raissa smiled and kissed Allegra on the cheek. "So tell me, do you have your flight booked?"

"I do!"

"To Spain?" Portia asked.

"Yes. I'm going for the half-term holiday. I can't wait!"

"I can't believe you and Jazz are both going to be deserting me and Hope," Portia said.

"Ah, uh, I think I'm going to be away too," Hope said. "My sister's invited me to come and visit her at her uni."

"No way!" Portia sighed as she crouched down to pet Nurey. "Ah well, at least my four-legged friends won't be deserting me."

Allegra giggled.

"And your friend with the bionic hip will still be here too," Raissa said. "I'm sure we'll be able to have some adventures while the others are away. There's so much I want to do now I'm mobile again." She put the kettle on and took some cups from the shelf.

"Let me do that for you," Allegra offered but Raissa shook her head.

"It's so nice to be able to move around freely again, I want to do it." She pointed at the table. "Sit down, please. Help yourself to a cake."

"Oh wow," Allegra exclaimed as she bit into one of the cakes and a delicious mixture of hazelnut and vanilla filled her mouth. "These are amazing."

"Thank you." Raissa smiled. "I used to make them when I was a girl, back in Moscow. You girls have really reminded me of those days. You've brought back so many happy memories."

Allegra took another bite of the cake and she looked around the table at the other girls, at Hope and Jazz chatting away, at Portia secretly feeding Nurey a treat, and she wondered what happy memories they were going to make together as the Moonlight Dreamers. Something told her there would be a lot, and this thought filled her with excitement.

Later that afternoon, after leaving Raissa, the girls made their way to the Palace Pier, where they bought hot chocolates to warm themselves against the autumn chill. Although the sun hadn't set yet, a pale crescent moon was just visible in the bright blue sky.

"I think we should all officially declare our dreams for the holiday," Jazz said as they sat on a bench overlooking the sea.

"Mine's easy," Allegra replied. "To have a wonderful Spanish adventure — and to eat my body weight in my abuela's paella!"

"Sounds awesome." Jazz grinned. "How about you, Hope?"

Hope looked out at the water shimmering beneath them. "My dream is to have fun staying with my sister at her uni – and not feel afraid."

"Great dream," Allegra said with a smile, placing her hand on Hope's arm.

"Portia?" Jazz asked.

"Hmm, well, I would have said that my dream is to not sulk about the fact that all of you will be off having amazing adventures while I'm stuck here on my own," Portia replied. "But I guess that's a little negative, and not what Oscar would want."

"Very true," Jazz agreed with a grin.

"So my dream is to find some stars to gaze at from my gutter while you're away. And I mean that metaphorically," she added. "I'm not going to spend the whole week staring at the sky. I need to find a new dream to focus on."

"I think I know something that might help – or rather, some*one*," Jazz replied, taking a book from her bag.

"Oscar!" Portia exclaimed.

"You know the drill," Jazz said, passing her the book. "Just hold it for a second and ask your question, then open it on a random page."

"Dear Oscar," Portia said dramatically, clutching the book to her chest, "now that I've tried rescuing a dog who didn't really need rescuing and ended up saving his owner instead, please tell me what I should dream of doing next."

The others all watched as she flicked the book open.

"What does it say?" Allegra asked as Portia read.

"It says, '*It is what you read when you don't have to that determines what you will be when you can't help it*'," Portia replied.

"Ooh, I like that!" Hope exclaimed.

"Me too," Allegra agreed.

"I'm glad I didn't get that one." Jazz laughed. "I don't read anything when I don't have to! But does it make sense to you?" She looked at Portia anxiously.

"Yes, it does." Portia grinned. "I think Oscar's telling me that my next dream should be to do with graphic novels. I'm obsessed with them."

"Awesome," Jazz replied.

"How about you, Jazz?" Hope asked. "What's your dream for the holiday?"

"Hmm, something tells me it will involve surfing," Portia teased.

"Damn right it does." Jazz looked up at the pale ghost of the moon watching down over them. "My dream is to surf every second I get while I'm in Cornwall."

"I can't wait till we meet again and find out how our dreams went," Allegra said.

"Me too." Jazz raised her cup of hot chocolate. "To the Moonlight Dreamers and all our adventures!"

The others raised their cups. "To the Moonlight Dreamers!"

"And Oscar," Portia added.

Best-selling, award-winning author **Siobhan Curham** has written more than forty books for adults, teenagers and children, including the internationally successful Moonlight Dreamers series. As a former council estate kid and university drop-out who very nearly gave up on her writing dream, Siobhan believes in helping as many people as possible achieve their own writing goals through her online writing community, The Writing Adventure.

You can find out more about Siobhan, her books and her writing projects at: www.siobhancurham.com

Twitter: @SiobhanCurham
Facebook: Siobhan Curham Author

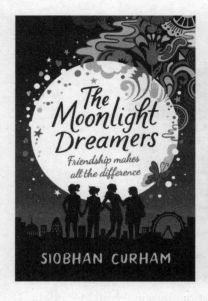
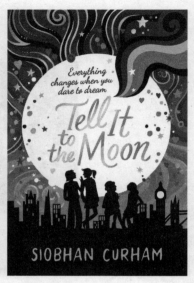

Meet the original Moonlight Dreamers:

Amber, Maali, Sky and Rose.

They're not like everyone else and they don't want to be.

Inspirational and heart-warming stories that celebrate
friendship and finding your place in the world.

#Moonlight Dreamers